D1553510

**Other Publications** by Dorothea are

Book:- "Enchantment Is Yours" A Journey of Spirit

Book:- Chakras" Introduction to the
Seven Major Energy Centers

CD:- Guided Meditation – Sacred Activation

CD:- Guided Meditation – Deep Relaxation

# *Pathways*

## TALES FOR EVERYONE

Enjoy your life. Peace,
Love & Blessings.

Dorothea Orleen Grant

**BALBOA**
PRESS
A DIVISION OF HAY HOUSE

Balboa Press books may be ordered through booksellers or by contacting:

Balboa Press
A Division of Hay House
1663 Liberty Drive
Bloomington, IN 47403
www.balboapress.com
1 (877) 407-4847

Printed in the United States of America.

ISBN: 978-1-4525-9356-2 (sc)
ISBN: 978-1-4525-9358-6 (hc)
ISBN: 978-1-4525-9357-9 (e)

Library of Congress Control Number: 2014903741

Balboa Press rev. date: 4/1/2014

# Dedication

This book is dedicated to
the "**Child**" in all
Humans.

# Reflections

Everything is fiction by authentic perception.

The human mind's perception turns it into what it likes.

********

Conscience is Sensible.

********

Silence is the most powerful sound.

Dorothea O Grant

# Preface

Everything communicates in its own language, rhythmic and musical vibrations.

Before there were words to communicate, and the alphabet, there were sounds, vibrations, symbols, and intentions. Yes, the most ancient language of humanity is in the form of sounds, vibrations, symbols, and intentions.

Currently, the most modern way for humans to communicate, in most cultures, is in language using the alphabet, and other symbols. The alphabet consists of twenty-six symbols called letters, from which words are formed and used by some humans to communicate. The letters of the alphabet are symbols.

My grandmother and my other ancestors before her used mostly the more ancient ways of communicating, and adapted to the modern ways over time.

My grandmother told me stories orally every night before bedtime. This was my most favorite part of the day. She would sit on the floor by the doorway, and I would sit under the blanket of the night sky, moon, and stars, facing her. As she told the story, I would make up visual representation of the story in my mind's eye. When I experience my grandmother's stories, I would dream that one day I would like to share storytelling with others. I found listening to stories entertaining, informative, fun, adventurous, exciting, magical, and sometimes scary.

So the first thing I set out to do as a child was to learn the alphabet, how to read, and write. I was successful at this, and even today, my most favorite thing to experience is reading and writing. Presently, writing is a magical art for me.

The most modern way to experience stories is through books. So in keeping with the most modern way of communication, I have created and written these stories to share with you, as my grandmother in the past shared with me. When I write, the vibrations of the stories flow through me, and I transform the vibrations into words to create stories.

My wish is that humans of all ages will read and enjoy the adventures of my writing, and use whatever they choose from these stories to enrich their lives. Take what you like from these stories, and with respect, quietly leave the rest on the pages undisturbed. Words are vibrations, and vibrations are alive.

Remember one of the most empowered and transformative activity in any part of the Universe is positive, enjoyable communication in thought, speech, action, or in any other form. You can develop the art of opening your heart to enjoying life in every step, every breath, and every story you create, as you live, and experience your life.

This book "Pathways" Tales For Everyone is a collection of five short stories. These stories can be enjoyed by children and the child in humans of all age. Through story telling people can discover many tools to learn and grow from and experience adventures and excitement. **Plus** as a bonus feature in this book there is a chapter on the awareness of the seven major energy centers called "Chakras."

# The stories are:-

## Love and the Toad

This is about the discovery of how love can magically help in the discovery of unexpected surprises, joy, and adventure, happiness, caring and sharing. Finding out the treasures that can be uncovered and discovered when unconditional love takes center stage between a girl Sunda and Drostan the toad.

## Love Finds A Way

This is a story about the adventure of two turkeys finding each other and falling in love. Through their strong, positive, and loving bond they survived many difficulties and created a family. Their story reminds us that dreams, prayer, and wishes can come true. And most of all, to always remember that love can find a way for things to end up positive.

## Ducky's Transformation

In this story, a duck really assisted and reinforced some of Anna's feelings about life. Sometimes, like this duck, we just have to choose to change our situation, or become open to change; to embrace fully what we desire the most; to believe in our desired intentions with all our hearts; to become aware that life is a story unfolding one step at a time; to discover the courage to take a chance and develop acceptance. Just like the beautiful colored duck, we can fly joyfully forward into the unknown with more trust and confidence.

## A Divine Partnership

This is a story about three passengers Spirit, Mind, and Body traveling in a Universal vehicle. Through difficulties they come to realize that working together in balanced partnership, can assist in accomplishing so much more. When this is done life can be positively productive, peaceful, and harmonious.

## The Three Tree Friends

The interesting and magical story of how two children Ned and Leila naturally on their own discovered the three tree friends of their parents and ancestors. The parents and trees with natural delight continue the traditional awareness and lessons of the three tree friends. The children are taught by their parents and the trees the legend of the three trees friends. Ned and Leila learned how the circle of life relationship between trees, and humans can be constructive and magical.

# Introduction to the Seven Major Chakras

*How does energy and information circulate in and out of the body?* The Chakras - are sometimes referred to as "wheel of light". They are very important in the operation of the human energetic system. The Chakras are junction points where energy and information circulates in and out of the body; depending on the person's experiences, both positive and negative. These awareness can assist in understanding the basic function of this energetic system. Becoming **"awaken"** to the Chakras can start what I call the journey home to understanding yourself.

*Life can be like a garden. You are the gardener of your life.*
*Take what you like and find useful from the garden of these stories, and leave the rest undisturbed. I enjoyed sharing my garden of stories with you.*

# Acknowledgement

Much gratitude: to my daughter Pia G. Pessoa for all her priceless contributions in the creation of this book. To my editor Renee Elizabeth-Anne Rewiski for her exceptional talents in editing this book.

Thank you for purchasing and reading my book.

Please recommend this book to someone else.

Enjoy your life.

Blessings Peace and Love to you.

Dorothea.

This is one of my tree friends.
Do you see her eyes?

# Contents

## Chapter One

# Love And The Toad

Once upon a time in a garden at a damp and isolated dark castle in Scotland, lived a cold-hearted toad in a cold pond. The toad was Prince Drostan, who was cursed by a fairy princess to live a long life as a toad for his uncaring, angry and mean ways. The spell could only be broken when he chose to genuinely love, become caring and affectionate from the heart, and to be loved. In the garden pond the other frogs, toads, and fishes would swim away when he came nearby. The pond creatures were fed up with the toad's negative ways and attempts to bully them. So it was difficult for him to make friends with the other pond creatures.

A beautiful peasant girl named Sunda lived in a small village close to the deserted old castle. Sunda lived with her father Ian, and mother Agnes. They were farmers. Sunda was sixteen years old and liked to wander off on her own during her free time after her daily chores. Plus, she had lots of time during the day to explore because she was on summer holidays away from school. Sunda was an only child. Sunda's closest friends were Jeff the fox and Glenda the blue jay.

Sunda had found Jeff in the woods when he was a baby. She took care of him so he became a pet friend of hers. When Jeff was a year old, she helped him adjust to living on his own in the woods like a normal fox. They were good friends, and sometimes spent time on many adventures. Glenda the blue jay flew from place to place and Sunda met her when she was taking a walk one day in the woods.

One day Sunda was on one of her usual adventures exploring in the woods. She had decided to go beyond the village to a path along a hillside that led deep within the forest. She walked and walked. It seemed to her over an hour had passed. Things started to look unfamiliar. She was lost and she knew it; very lost. She had taken the wrong path. But the trees and surroundings seemed to get more and more mysterious.

"This is interesting," she thought to herself. "I should not go any further," she decided. "I should retrace my steps and find my way out of the forest back to where the path was familiar to me," she said out loud. As she continued to walk through the enchanted forest, she came upon a dark and damp old castle covered with green moss and vines. Every plant around the castle as far as the eyes could see was overgrown. Sunda wondered what this place could have been, and who might be living in it. The castle looked deserted but she slowly crept up to the large front door, which was opened a little, cleared some creeping vines away; slowly and cautiously she pushed the door open and peeked in.

Sunda held her breath from the musty bitter smell, and shivered as a very cold feeling swept over her from head to feet. Sunda called out through the darkness "HELLO! HELLO IS ANY ONE HERE!" but there was no answer, so she quickly left.

"It was not a good idea to explore this castle by myself. I must find the path back to where I began. I am hungry and tired. The sun is way up in the sky. It must be past lunchtime. I am thirsty. I will return tomorrow with Jeff after my morning chores," Sunda said.

She had to find her way out of the forest. Sunda figured her way out of the forest and arrived home breathless, tired, thirsty, and hungry. The first thing she did was drink lots of water, then had something to eat.

After lunch she took a nap. Being so tired she fell into a very deep sleep. Her mother was busy doing the laundry.

That night when Sunda lay in bed she thought about the dark, musty, smelly, and mysterious castle. She wondered what was the uneventful, sad, but enchanting feeling that seemed to be beckoning her and compelling her to enter, and to venture within its dark womb. She said to herself out loud "What lies within this seemingly doomed castle." She fell asleep that night after telling herself that she would return to the castle the next day.

It was a cloudy day when Sunda woke up the next morning. The sun was hiding behind layers of clouds. She went about doing her chores as quickly as she could. "Mother," she said, "I am going for my walk in the woods." "OK!" her mother replied loudly. Sunda's father had already set out early in the morning to take the goats, sheep, and cows with Denny the dog to the green pasture in the valley. Denny was a good shepherd dog. Sunda loved excitement, adventure, mystery, and exploration. Some feelings were still beckoning her to return to the castle. Although Sunda wanted to return to the castle, she was scared to go back alone.

"I will stop to see my friend Jeff the fox on my way to the castle. He could be my company, and maybe he will have some suggestions on how to go about visiting the castle again," Sunda said out loud to herself. Jeff the fox was sly, wise, adventurous, and seemed to be filled with bright ideas. Walking along for about fifteen minutes, Jeff the fox sneaked up behind Sunda, "Hi, there, and how are you today?" asked Jeff slyly. "I am fine Jeff," said Sunda. She then continued to tell him about the castle she had discovered.

Jeff decided to go with Sunda to the castle. They stopped to drink some water at the rolling brook, and to eat plums from a tree that was along the way.

Sunda and Jeff arrived at the castle. Sunda slowly and cautiously pushed the door open, and Jeff the fox crept in cautiously by Sunda's side. "Wow it sure stinks in here," said Jeff. Sunda agreed. The cold dank smell and the grey darkness of the castle sent shivers up Sunda's spine. They looked around the castle slowly. They cautiously started at the entrance. The windows and beautiful furniture were all covered with moss, dust, and spider webs. Very creepy.

Out of nowhere there was a rustling sound of papers and leaves. When Sunda looked down on the floor it was covered with paper and leaves. Running from under the paper, which littered the floor, was a fast movement. A white mouse ran hurriedly into a hole in the wall next to a beautiful yellow chair. A majestic looking harp was sitting sideways on the yellow chair. All of a sudden another mouse leaped out of the yellow chair from under the harp. It almost landed on Sunda's foot. Sunda shivered and jumped back, screaming "HELP! HELP ME!"

The fox jumped to her side and said, "I think we should leave now." Sunda agreed.

She hurried towards a window close to the front door. She cleaned off the window with the bottom of her dress. Sunda found the lock to the window and hurriedly pushed it open. This, she thought, would let in some fresh air, and sunlight. Sunda decided she would visit the castle again the next day. Something mysterious and magical seemed to be enticing her to return, she kept thinking.

She had the feeling of leaving but also the sense of returning, and staying. Jeff the fox was already out the door. "Jeff you are supposed to be brave. You seemed so scared," Sunda said.

"Oh, I am so thirsty. Come on let's go get some water by the brook," said Jeff skillfully avoiding what Sunda had said.

The next morning when Sunda awoke the sun was bright and hot. Everything seemed to smile with golden rays of life.

Sunda did her usual chores, and set off for the mysterious castle. She wanted to know what laid within and who owned the castle. Sunda was very curious, fearless and courageous. She met her friend Jeff the fox on her way. He was waiting for her by the brook. Jeff was busily eating ripe plums that lay limp and lifeless on the ground. Sunda picked some plums for herself, which she ate as they walked along. Within minutes she quickened her pace and hurriedly they journeyed to the castle. Having her friend the fox with her provided comforting support. Jeff was known to be sly, and fearless, but after his actions yesterday at the castle, Sunda began to doubt this. But, to her, having her friend with her was better than going to the castle all by herself.

They arrived at the castle and everything seemed the same as yesterday, except that the sun's rays were peeking cautiously through the open window, and the air was not as stagnant as the day before. The castle felt distant, sad, cold, dark and mysterious. What story could have lain within these walls, she thought? Sunda opened as many windows as she could and slowly more sunlight and air penetrated the castle. The slight freshness of the air and sunlight coming in seemed to bring renewed life to the inside of the castle.

Sunda could see much more clearly inside the room. Dust about a half-inch thick was laying on the floor and furniture. With every step, dust rose from the floor like clouds surrounding her legs. The fox walked slowly and quietly beside her with his tail held high in the air as if trying to avoid the dust.

There were many spider webs and spiders on the ceiling, furniture, walls, and mirrors. The castle seemed to have been empty for many years. A lonely silence filled the air. Sunda and Jeff the fox shivered as a chilly breeze crept slowly by them.

"This is very creepy. I wonder where the breeze was coming from," asked the fox. "Very creepy indeed," replied Sunda.

They were deeper into the castle passing what seemed to be a dining hall. There were two rooms off to the right of the dining hall and a window was slightly open. They entered this room. It was a kitchen.

"Let us check out the backyard," said Jeff. "Ok, let us go through the kitchen in the back. There is a door that I think leads to the backyard," said Sunda. Jeff could not wait to get outside; the creepy feeling of the castle was giving him shivers.

Sunda passed through the kitchen cautiously with Jeff the fox leading the way. There were cobwebs, spiders, dust, and many things littering the floor of the kitchen. Sunda found the back door to the kitchen, and pushed it open.

They stepped outside into the sun and looked around for some place to sit. They found the fresh air outside welcoming and very refreshing. Sunda and Jeff the fox sat down on a bench outside the door. They felt tired and sleepy from the dusty atmosphere within the enclosed castle.

After a little rest they stood up and stepped out into the yard. They were surprised to see a beautiful but tangled garden filled with wild flowers, tall grass, and butterflies of many sizes and colors busily flying around. Birds were chirping as they too moved from branch to branch of trees. Things seemed to suddenly come alive.

They walked along a brick pathway that led to the center of the garden. There they found a magnificent, huge pond with lily pads the size of large trays. Bright pink, yellow, and green butterflies were busily flying around in a wonderful dance. The neglected garden had a magical cheerfulness to it. Jeff the fox was busily looking around for animals to catch and eat for lunch.

Sunda felt hungry and tired. "Jeff I am so tired let us leave, and tomorrow we will return to explore this garden. I will meet you at our usual place by the brook," said Sunda. Jeff agreed. He did not find food and he was tired and hungry too. On the way home Sunda and Jeff talked about their day's adventure. Sunda returned home.

She got something to eat and took an afternoon nap. During her sleep she had many visions. She was talking in her sleep with so much excitement her mother noticed and woke her up.

"Are you all right?" Sunda's mother asked her. "I am fine, just dreaming," said Sunda. She did not want to tell her mother about her discovery. This deserted castle was her adventure and she was not going to take a chance on having the experience taken away by her parents telling her not to go back there.

Sunda helped her mother with milking the goats, and preparing food for supper. It was now late afternoon and the sun was almost setting. Her father would be arriving home soon. He usually went away after breakfast to work on the farm and to attend to the animals. Her mother stayed in the home to attend to her chores and Sunda most times helped her with the chores.

Sunda was a dreamer; she loved to daydream and sleep dream. That night she had many dreams. As she slept that night she tossed and turned so much that she fell out of bed. It was as if she were a fish swimming in a violent storm at sea. Sunda's castle adventure was spilling over in her sleep dream. One time she woke up suddenly not sure where she was. She shook her head from side to side, and glanced around her room in the dark. She saw that she was home and in her room. She went back to sleep after using her sheets to tuck herself securely into her bed to prevent herself from falling out again.

The next morning Sunda woke up earlier than usual. It was her chore that morning to take the goats to a grass meadow close to her home to graze for the day. After breakfast she helped her mother to prepare and pack her father's lunch. Sunda's father gave her a kiss on the forehead and set out for the farm. Sunda completed her chores. She then said goodbye to her mother.

"Where are you going today?" her mother asked. "I am going up the hill to play with my friend Jeff. We found a beautiful garden in the back of a deserted castle," Sunda replied.

"Be careful, and remember to get the goats from the pasture before your father gets home," her mother called out to her as she scampered out the door. Sunda's curiosity was motivating her forward into the unknown.

Sunda met Jeff the fox and they hurried to the garden at the back of the castle. They entered the garden through a gate they found the day before when they were leaving. Sunda was curiously looking at the lily pads on the water in the pond. They were the largest she had ever seen. They were so green and strong. Sunda touched one of the lily pad as if checking to see if it was real.

SPLASH! CROAK! CROAK! came a loud noise. Sunda jumped back from the side of the pond. She fell over backwards. Then she sat up to see a huge toad sitting in the center of the pond on a lily pad. The lily pad seemed like a bright green stool.

"Wow you startled me," said Sunda to the toad.

"What are you doing here?" asked the toad to Sunda in a mean, cold, choking voice. The toad kept leaping on the lily pads closer and closer as he came towards Sunda.

Sunda became afraid upon hearing and seeing the toad coming closer. To her he looked slimy, with lumpy skin, and big eyes that stared at her intensely. Sunda backed up slowly, then faster. She suddenly turned and called out to Jeff who was nowhere in sight.

"JEFF! Jeff! Jeff! let's go!"

Jeff came running over to Sunda. His mouth was covered in wild berry juice. Sunda told Jeff what had happen. Jeff looked and saw the big slimy toad. The toad was hopping towards them from lily pad to lily pad. Sunda dashed through the garden as if being chased. Jeff the fox was close behind her, and he ran past her without hesitation. They ran through the garden into the woods.

Sunda ran all the way home. Jeff continued into the woods as if being chased. After lunch and a nap Sunda helped her mother with the ironing of the clothes, and then went to get the goats from the pasture.

All night the scary vision of the ugly toad seemed to fill Sunda's mind and dreams. She tossed and turned all night, sometimes waking up covered in sweat. Her dreams were more active and colorful. She tucked herself into her bed but she still kept falling out.

"Wow what a night," she said out loud when she woke up the next morning. "I have some thinking to do," she said.

That morning Sunda did not go to the castle; she was too afraid. Ten days had passed and Sunda did not return to visit the castle. Every day the toad came up from the bottom of the pond and sat on his lily pad to wait for Sunda. He wondered where the beautiful girl had appeared from, and disappeared to. He silently wished that she would return, so that he could have a friend. He waited, and waited, and waited. The toad had not seen a human in so many years. He sadly went to bed each evening, sometimes sobbing. He hardly ate. The toad felt even lonelier than before. He left like he could have jumped out of his skin with anticipation wondering if Sunda would return. Along with all of this he found everything and everyone in the pond even more annoying. He felt so irritated and sad.

Sunda kept busy. Then one day her friend Glenda the blue jay came to visit her as she sat by the brook daydreaming. Sunda told Glenda about the castle. Glenda the blue jay knew the castle. She lived in the forest and had seen it many times. Sunda also told Glenda about the ugly and mean-looking toad. Sunda said to Glenda "I need help deciding if I should return to the castle."

Glenda the blue jay suggested Sunda should go back to the castle garden to visit the toad. Glenda told Sunda that she would go with her. Although Sunda was scared and hesitant, they set out in the direction of the castle. Sunda asked Glenda, "What good could come out of caring about an old toad that seems to know only the cold pond? I wonder why I seem to care so much. I cannot get him out of my mind no matter how hard I try; he even shows up in my dreams. OH Glenda why, why, why?"

To Sunda the toad looked mean; he had a loud angry, domineering voice that scared her like thunder banging against the sky on a dark night. "Sunda you might be able to answer your questions by going back to the castle garden to visit the toad," said Glenda.

They arrived at the castle. In the pond close to the edge, the toad was sitting quietly on a rock looking very lonely and sad. Glenda flew towards the toad and said, "hi mister toad, how are you today?" The toad looked up startled. He was surprised and happy at the same time to see them, especially Sunda.

Sunda stood nervously and curiously about six feet from the pond, looking steadily at the toad and Glenda. In a very deep voice the toad said: "I am sad, hungry and my heart aches. Can I come home with you?" He asked Sunda.

She said "OH! no way!"

Glenda the blue jay told Sunda that maybe she can help the toad by putting him in the small pond by the brook close to where she lived. Sunda, in a quivering voice, replied, "How would he get there, and the pond had no lily pads, few fish, no frog or toad friends, and just boulders to sit on."

The toad said, "I do not mind because it would be better than being in the castle pond. I would eat bugs, and sometimes get to see you more." The toad told them that he could get to the other pond by hopping along behind Sunda, on the way to the pond by her home. Sunda was hesitant.

Sunda said "I guess it would not hurt to help the toad if he promised not to hurt me." The toad in a humble low voice said, "I promise to be good." Sunda suggested that it would be better if she carried him in a container instead of him hopping along behind her or beside her because she was worried that maybe she would accidentally step on him.

Sunda left to look in the castle's kitchen if she could find a container big enough for the toad to fit in and also easy for her to carry. With courage she found a big pot in the kitchen, brought it to the pond, laid it sideways, and the toad happily jumped inside. The toad promised to be quiet and to try not to scare Sunda, to work on becoming friendly and kind. The toad said to Sunda and Glenda, "I will work on my coarse and deep scary voice as well by singing, and thinking kind thoughts. I will over time transform my negative ways."

With Sunda cautiously carrying the big pot with the toad, and Glenda flying ahead, they set off for the pond close to Sunda's home. For the whole journey, the toad kept very quiet. When they arrived at the pond Sunda gently placed the pot on the ground by the edge of the pond. She tilted the pot carefully to one side and the toad happily jumped out of the pot and into the pond with a splash. "Thank you sooooo much," the toad said to Sunda and Glenda. Sunda and Glenda left after staying with the toad for a little while.

Days and many full moons went by and the toad got used to his new home in the small pond by the rambling brook. He loved hearing the music of the brook, which helped him with his singing. His deep voice began to lighten up to a sweet mellow tone.

Sunda, the blue jay, and the fox came to visit the toad every day. Slowly Sunda and the toad became friends; she began to trust him, and to become more comfortable with him. They would exchange stories and laugh at one another's jokes. The toad also had learned how to whistle, and he sang for them when his voice became more pleasant.

Sometimes they all sang together. The toad began to beam with excitement, kindness, and joy. After seven full moons, Sunda became fond of the toad. He would hop along side her on some of her walks in the woods and gradually they even became best of friends. Sunda's love and trust towards the toad gradually grew each day. Sunda's kind-heartedness seemed to have rubbed off on the toad, and he became sincerely happy, content and at peace. The toad enjoyed this experience he had never known before.

Sunda started to take the toad into her home, in her big apron pocket. The toad liked this very much and he promised to be quiet so that her parents would not know he was inside her pocket. He loved being in Sunda's pocket. Her pockets felt like a warm sunlit pouch. Being so close to her made him feel safe and cared for. The toad grew to genuinely love Sunda.

After Sunda's chores, sometimes she would lie by the brook resting. She like the sound the water made as it busily rolled over, around and through the brook, like a musical band. One day as Sunda lay asleep by the brook the toad hopped up to Sunda's face licked it with his firm tongue, and kissed her. His love for her had blossomed naturally to an irresistible feeling of joy and contentment.

Sunda woke up startled; she had felt his kiss. To her surprise, standing before her was a very handsome young man. She was so surprised to find this glowing young man dressed like a prince. He looked like someone who often showed up in her dreams, day and night.

"Who are you?" Sunda asked. "I am the toad," said Drostan. "I have waited so long for the spell of the fairy queen to be reversed. Thank you so much for helping me to change the spell. Our warm heartedness and loving kindness was the secret antidote to my past, and transforming back into a prince."

Growing up, Sunda often wished one day she would meet a handsome prince, fall in love, get married and live in a beautiful castle. This was a dream opposite to the life she knew and lived in the beautiful valley with her forest friends and parents. The young prince told her of his story and the curse of the fairy princess. He asked Sunda to return to the castle with him. He thanked her for helping him to break the curse.

Sunda told her parents of her secret friend the toad, and how he has returned to being a human. Sunda, Jeff, and Glenda went with Drostan to show him the way back to his old home the castle.

Drostan returned to the castle and found the treasures he had hidden within the castle. He spent the next three years fixing the castle and readjusting to life again as a human living in the castle. At the castle all the moss on the windows, the creepy vines, dust, and cobwebs in the castle and yard, had disappeared. The castle had been transformed into a warm sunlit magical palace. The gardens were magnificent and everything had come to life as if with the wave of a magic wand. There were carriages, servants, coachmen, cooks, and everything that their hearts desired for living in a castle. The sound of laughter was everywhere. Sunda, Glenda the blue jay, and Jeff the fox visited Drostan, and they all became good friends.

Another year passed and Drostan asked Sunda to be his wife. He promised her a life of love, affluence and joy. Sunda happily agreed. Her dream had come true.

Through her unconditional love, he found love and thus found himself. She agreed to spend the rest of her life with the prince in his castle and be his princess and best friend.

Within a month after the wedding announcement, there was a magnificent wedding for Drostan and Sunda, followed by a huge wedding feast and a fantastic ball. They got married and became the happy prince and princess of the enchanted castle. Prince Drostan and princess Sunda lived happily ever after. They shared their joy with their three children and everyone both near and far. With each year they met many people as their life unfolded like a magical carpet of heavenly bliss. They grew together even deeper in love. And Sunda's parent Ian and Agnes sold their farm and moved into the castle with Drostan and Sunda.

Love can magically fill the most impossible situation when you least expect it with surprises, joy, adventure, happiness, caring and sharing.

So remember the next time you see a toad, or encounter an unpleasant situation, smile and radiate an open heart filled with love and kindness. You never know what treasures love can uncover and discover.

You might be very surprised at what can magically appear right before your very eyes. And also remember dreams really can come true when you plant the seeds of your intentions and desires within the enchanted magical garden of unconditional love and radiant sunshine.

When you least expect it, love can magically fill the most impossible situation with surprises, joy, adventure, happiness, caring, sharing, and lots of light to brighten your way.

### The End

## Chapter Two

# Love Finds A Way

W ild turkeys do not like thanksgiving celebrations, dining rooms, tables, stoves, people, utensils, pots, or, as a matter of fact, anything that has to do with humans, their lives, including their homes, and being caged. Wild turkeys like to live free in nature. Tanka the turkey lives in the wild and tangled forest with her parents, brothers, and sisters. They roam freely every day, but most important to them is keeping a watchful eye for humans who would like to catch them, especially close to Thanksgiving and Christmas Day.

Tanka dreamed of being in a different forest, but she also knew that it was wise to stay in the environment that was familiar to her, and in the protective safety of her family. Early one morning as the sun started to peek into the forest Tanka woke up from her nest of dried leaves and branches. She shook off sleepy stillness, stretched and flapped her wings, looking around curiously.

She had heard a strange crackling of tree branches and a familiar loud noise. Tanka looked close to where she was standing and saw her parents and brothers and sisters were still sleeping. "What can that noise be?" Tanka asked as she cautiously stepped through the opening in the bushes and tangled bamboo plant leaves to see as far as her long neck could glide. "What had made that familiar noise?" Tanka questioned.

"HELLO!" "How are you today?" asked a strange voice. Tanka turned around quickly; she was surprised to find a big turkey standing on a huge rock.

"Well hello there, and who are you?" asked Tanka.

"My name is Kizi and I am very happy to see you," Kizi said flapping his wings excitedly.

"Be quiet. My parents, brothers and sisters are still sleeping," Tanka told this new turkey, annoyed that he dropped in uninvited. She had never seen this turkey before; her family was the only flock living in the forest as far as she knew. "What now?" asked Tanka.

Without giving any more attention to this stranger, Tanka decided to go on her usual morning errand to gather food within her stomach for her breakfast. Kizi followed her making sure to keep some distance behind her; he thought she did not seem too friendly. When she stopped, he stopped. He did not look in her direction but pretended to be digging in the earth, or looking in another direction, just in case she tried to chase him away. They continued avoiding each other for a while, until Tanka decided to go back into the direction she came from. As she went by Kizi, she invited him to come back with her to meet her family. Surprised Kizi said "Ok."

Tanka's family consisted of seven turkeys, including her. Tanka and her family did not have any young babies because wild predators had eaten all their eggs. When Tanka returned to her family's sleeping nest, her family was awake flapping their wings, as if stretching, and making a throbbing screeching noise. They shuffled around as if in a hurry for something very important.

"It is time for a yummy breakfast and exercise," said Gus, Tanka's father. Off everyone ran quickly flapping their wings as they followed Gus.

Scratching and pulling insects and worms from the earth was their first and most enjoyable thing to do in the morning. Tanka's father Gus invited Kizi to join their family and to live with them. Kizi said, "thank you I am so happy."

One day Tankas and Kizi were walking in the forest when they bumped into the Forest Ranger. The Forest Ranger stopped when he saw the both of them and took a closer look at Kizi. The Ranger noticed Kizi had a silver tag on his right foot. Wild turkeys in the forest are not tagged. Tanka and Kizi noticed the Forest Ranger and they ran very quickly into the forest.

Kizi seemed very anxious and worried. Tanka asked Kizi, "What? Why do you seem so afraid?"

Kizi then told Tanka his story, and why he was in this forest. Part of Kizi's life story was that he was hit by a car and broke his right hip in a town many miles away. Kizi was taken to a Wild Life Environmental Center in the same town. The park attendants there fixed his injuries, put his leg and hip in a support cast. Kizi healed over time. But from being confined in a cage for so long he was considered not able to live and survive in the wild any more. Kizi showed Tanka the silver looking tag on his foot.

"Oh my, you must hide," said Tanka. Kizi hid in the forest with Tanka's family from late summer to fall of the following year.

Kizi was very happy being with Tanka and her family, feeling at home and no longer alone. At the Wild Life Environmental Center, Kizi used to live in a circular fenced in area with no roof and a pond in the center. Kizi lived as roommates with one female peacock, two male peacocks, some mandarin ducks who often visited, two turtles and Canadian geese who would stop in from time to time. Kizi was good friends with the peacocks. He missed them but was happier free and in the wild with Tanka and her family.

As time went by, Tanka and Kizi developed a very close intimate relationship. The fall season arrived with a blanket of chill, frost, and rain. With frozen attitudes, the turkeys built nests from dried broken branches and leaves. They made their cozy nests up and into the branches of large trees, away from humans and predators. They snuggled up night and day to keep warm and cozy, especially when it snowed. Fall and winter were the most difficult times for them. During the holiday seasons, for which turkeys were used as food, were stressful times for Tanka and her family. They had to be extra cautious that they did not end up as food during the holidays of Thanksgiving and Christmas.

Kizi learned from Tanka and her family many hiding and escaping techniques. He learned how to camouflage, duck, run, hide, and find food. Kizi thought the experience of being with these turkeys was priceless.

"Thank you so much for everything," Kizi said to Tanka and her family early one morning as they strolled along through the bushes looking for food. Kizi was learning to function in the wild as a turkey again. Kizi also thought, "great, this was my dream."

But the bitter chill of winter seemed endless to Kizi. Sometimes he was cold to the bones. From time to time he wondered about his friends back at the Environmental Center — the peacocks, ducks, turtles and geese — he missed them. Kizi also thought that experiencing his first winter in the wild made life at the Environmental Center seem like a resort hotel. Kizi from time to time missed the warmth of his winter enclosed cage, access to food and water, and rest. At the Center there was not much room to walk around in the winter enclosed cage, but he still missed being there. Kizi was having many mixed feelings.

During the winter at the Environmental Center, Kizi, the two male and one female peacock were moved to an enclosed cage with a roof. The cage also had a heating system and park attendants always arrived daily to feed them. During the fall through to early spring the wings of the peacocks and Kizi were not clipped. There was no need to because the cage they were living in had a roof that stopped them from flying away. From spring to fall the peacocks and Kizi had their wings clipped and trimmed so that they would not fly out of the top of their cage and leave the Environmental Center. The peacocks and Kizi would fly up and out of the cage if the park attendant forgot to clip and trim their wings. Clipping and trimming Kizi's wings caused him to lose some of his natural flying confidence and ability as a wild turkey.

Kizi was again reflecting on his past life at the Center. He remembered that he was injured and confined in an enclosed cage with no other turkey to have turkey conversations and connections with. Sometimes he would dream that things would be different and that he was free and had turkey friends. Kizi also dreamed of having a family. He had grown to turkey adulthood. Kizi's dream of being free and being with other turkeys came through at the end of spring that year. And now here he was with Tanka and her family.

When Kizi was at the Center day after day, he continued his dreaming. Kizi was feeling great, but longed to be in the wild, free to continue his life as a wild turkey. Kizi knew he might not find his family that he was with before the accident. Kizi wanted to escape after being caged for eighteen months, almost his entire life. His wild turkey desires kept bubbling up. Kizi developed the courage and planned the escape from the Center with the first opportunity.

Spring had arrived with welcoming joy for Kizi. Being cooped up was difficult for him. Not having his wings clipped and trimmed during the winter created a great opportunity for Kizi to escape. Kizi knew this, so he waited and stayed focused.

During the spring, he was transferred from his winter cage back to the roofless spring to fall cage. Kizi thought this would be a great opportunity. Wings not clipped and trimmed, Kizi thought again and again that this would help him move faster. It was spring and the park attendant came to transfer them. The attendant came with four separate cages, one for each of them.

"Ok! This could be the big opportunity," thought Kizi. The cages were brought inside the larger cage, and each of the birds was placed in separate cages. "Oh no, this might not be a good time to escape," said Kizi as he observed what the attendant was doing.

Kizi and the peacocks were taken to the large cage. The attendant forgot to close the gate of the large cage when she entered with the last small cage. Kizi was in this cage. When she let Kizi out of the small cage, Kizi ran between her legs and dashed out of the cage door. Kizi ran and ran as fast as his legs could move. He felt as if he had on roller skates. Soon Kizi remembered that he could fly. So he flapped his wings very fast as he ran. Running and flying, Kizi left the Environmental Center way behind. This is how Kizi made his grand escape.

Although Kizi had mixed feelings he was happy to put life at the Environmental Center in the past. Life with Tanka and her family was more than he could ever wish for. Sometimes in many ways it was difficult for Kizi to get used to being free and in the wild. It was now spring in the forest with Tanka and her family. Kizi decided to renew and improve his attitude.

The bond between Tanka and Kizi had gotten to the point where they choose each other as partners and mates for the season, bringing new life to the turkey species. Spring was springing into bloom. Leaves peeked out of branches, new flower buds emerged, chipmunks and squirrels ran back and forth. The sunlight streamed through tree branches like flowing water. Birds flew and chirped joyful tunes. Turkeys in the forest, Jennies, Toms and Jakes gave off their mating calls. Responding female turkeys made a sound like keowk, keowk to any available male. Male turkeys would gobble in response. The forest vibrations were of very mixed expressions from the turkey family of Tanka, Kizi and other turkeys who came into the forest for Spring's mating celebration making sounds of gobble, boom, yelp, cluck, putt, purr, whine, cackle, and kee-kee. The female and male turkeys were noisy as they called back and forth to one another.

Tanka and Kizi had already chosen each other, but Tanka stood her ground and made Kizi court her. Kizi tried to impress her with mating calls, opening and shaking his wings and tail. Kizi opened up his feathers spread his wings and tail, puffed up his feathers and dragged his wings on the ground strutting around her. Kizi's brightly colored head and neck showed red, blue and white and changed color depending on his mood. When he was most excited his neck was a solid, mostly white color. Tanka played hard to get, seemingly ignoring Kizi as she wandered around. Female turkeys mate with the strongest and most impressive male to ensure a healthy brood of children that will survive in the wild or survive in general.

Tanka most times was busy eating as Kizi did his mating impressions. She would eat acorns, nuts, tree bark, chestnut, hickory, pinyon pine, seeds, insects, berries, roots, small snakes and grass. Tanka knew she had to fill up on nutrition for mating, laying good quality eggs, and hatching them; she had to survive and may have to fast while sitting on her eggs, waiting for them to hatch.

Hatching would take about twenty-eight days, and she may not be able to go too far from her eggs. She would have to stay sitting on her eggs, or very close by, to prevent predators like raccoons, opossums, skunks, foxes, groundhogs, rodents, snakes, eagles and hawks from eating her eggs or babies.

When Tanka was ready, she mated with Kizi. When Tanka was finished mating, she looked for a nesting site. She was very secretive, distancing herself from the other turkeys. Tanka found the spot she liked. It was hidden by a large section of bushes and tall grass.

Tanka and Kizi built the nest together by collecting leaves, twigs and other vegetation. When the nest was complete Tanka laid an egg each day for nine days. She had nine brown-speckled eggs. She sat on the eggs keeping them as warm as possible for an incubation journey of about twenty-eight days. Kizi would bring her food sometimes, or she would leave for short periods while Kizi would sit on the eggs for her until she returned.

By now it was late spring. One day Kizi went out to search for food and did not return to be with Tanka. Tanka sat and sat, wondering and worrying, even more so as it began to get dark, "where was Kizi?" she wondered. "Very unusual," she thought, plus she was very hungry. "I should go see if I can find Kizi, I will not go too far from the nest, and I will also get something to eat," Tanka said sadly. She covered the eggs with some dried leaves and left.

After sitting on the eggs all day without eating, Tanka felt like a robot that needed oil; she could hardly walk and felt dizzy. Tanka did not see Kizi. She ate and returned to her nest of eggs. There was a little chill in the air, and it rained a little overnight.

With no Kizi to help keep her warm, for the first time in a long time she felt extra cold. Worrying all night as to what had happened to Kizi had made her restless that she hardly slept.

Poor Kizi! When he had gone in search of food, to his surprise the Park Ranger and a park attendant had found Kizi. They caught him with a big net. From the first time the Park Ranger saw Kizi, he alerted the park attendants to catch him at the best opportunity. Today was the day.

Kizi was caught. He was scared, frustrated, and tried his best to escape, but could not. Kizi thought about Tanka sitting on the eggs waiting for his return.

"Oh no, this is a very big disaster," said Kizi. If there was ever a time Kizi wanted to speak the human language, it was today. He wished he could explain his story and whole situation to the park attendant. The park attendant read the information on the silver tag on Kizi's foot. The silver tag noted where he was from, so Kizi was taken back to the Environmental Center that he was living in before escaping to the forest.

Kizi was placed in the open roof cage with his friends the peacocks. The Environmental Center attendant clipped Kizi's wings to ensure that he did not escape. Kizi was sad, very sad. The peacocks wanted to hear of Kizi's escape adventure, but he was too sad and traumatized to say one gobble. Kizi just laid down staring into space with the most blank facial expression; not one single gobble did Kizi express. He felt depressed and hardly ate. He ignored his old friends, and they wondered why he was so sad.

Tanka hatched her nine eggs. She now had five jakes, which are male, and four jennies, which are female turkeys, to take care of. Although the children grew very quickly, preventing them from being eaten by predators was one very difficult task. Tanka also had to teach her children how to survive: what to eat, how to communicate, and how and where they would sleep day and night. Tanka was very concerned; she thought about Kizi very often but with her responsibilities keeping her busy, the memories of Kizi and their time together slowly drifted out of her thoughts. "For now I must become focused on keeping these children safe and alive," she told herself.

Tanka still had the company of her father Gus, her mother Mamaro, plus her brothers and sisters. Everyone was busy with their responsibilities of raising their newly hatched children. There was an inner natural communication within their turkey network on keeping their species multiplying. The force of mother and father nature guides them forward.

Tanka kept very busy with raising her brood. She stayed mostly in the dense grassy field or in much wooded areas. Occasionally she would go out into the open field with her children. During the night when it was dark was the most difficult to protect her brood from predators. By late summer, even with Tanka's magnificent efforts to protect her children, she only had three surviving children left.

When Tanka's children were young a huge hawk had swooped down and grabbed one. Raccoons, a fox, and a groundhog had eaten the other five during the night when they were sleeping. Tanka was always late in stopping their attempts to steal her children. In nature it is survival of the strongest, and Tanka knew this. Tanka is sad about the children who were eaten, but kept her attention and focus on the ones she still had to prevent from being eaten, too. She was comforted knowing her family was still around.

The essence of fall was in the air. Tanka's two jakes and one jenny had grown. Tanka could now relax. Her responsibilities as a parent were now complete, except for having to guide her children on how to prepare the nest for the late fall and winter. Tanka stayed in the flock of her parents, brothers and sister and their children for the fall and winter. They built their nest in some trees deep in the forest.

During the fall and winter, Tanka strolled around looking sad and lonely. She daydreamed a lot about Kizi and their time together. It was the time they met last year. Oh, how she wondered what had happened to Kizi and wished he was with her now. She wanted very much for him to see the children. She thought maybe Kizi was caught and taken back to the place he told her he escaped from; she sighed, she wondered, she daydreamed.

Tanka's urge to find Kizi got stronger and stronger. But she knew setting out with the children, leaving the safety and warmth of her flock during the winter, was not a good idea. She knew that around this time was the most dangerous for turkeys to be killed and eaten by humans. It was the holiday season; Thanksgiving was around the corner, followed by Christmas.

Tanka was born in the wild, in the forest. She was an expert on how to survive, and she also knew the wisdom of staying alive. She knew about turkeys and what happens to turkeys around the holiday season. The story of turkeys and humans was a traditional story passed down from parent turkeys to their children. Tanka decided that very early in spring of the following year she would take the children, leave the forest and her family flock to find Kizi. The thought of leaving the forest scared her, but she had decided that she must go to find Kizi.

One day during the winter, Tanka told her children the story about how she met their father, how he disappeared, and why she was taking them in early spring to find him. After telling her children, she felt more at ease, not as sad as she did before. Tanka was even now more focused on planning her trip by daydreaming. She remembered from Kizi's story where he said he came from, and she had ideas on how to find the Environmental Center. She thought if Kizi found her, then it was possible for her to find him.

Spring began to peek out from behind the cold and dampness of winter. Tanka told her family she was leaving to find Kizi. Tanka's family did not think this was a good idea, but they respected and understood Tanka's decision. Tanka left the forest with her three children.

Tanka and the children would fly during the daylight, stop in wooded areas to eat and rest until late evening. She and the children would walk, run and hide as they traveled during the night. At night she thought she was safest from being caught by a human. The roads were less busy with cars at night so the roads were less dangerous. But at night she had to be cautious of predators too.

She kept her children close beside her or guided them to walk quickly in front of her. Tanka traveled for five days and nights. She had gotten over her fears as she got used to the experiences of the journey. Her fears of danger seemed to just drift away each day. She became an expert traveler with her children, flying, hiding, resting, eating, and crossing the street.

With these experiences, Tanka's children grew up quickly and became more and more brave and strong.

On the morning of the sixth day of Tanka's travels, she arrived at this place. To her it looked like a forest, but everything seemed organized. Grass was cut, trees were planted in organized groups, deer were wandering around, and different animals scampered about. Tanka also saw many Canadian geese and mandarin ducks. What caught her attention most were some different kinds of animals in cages — foxes, owls, hawks, deer, and an eagle.

"Wow, I think I have found where Kizi lived. I wonder if he is here?" Tanka thought. She saw attendants feeding the foxes, and she ran with her children to hide behind some bushes. When she thought the attendant could not see them, she ran quickly by. Her intention was to look around carefully to see if she saw Kizi.

Kizi had told Tanka he stayed in a circular cage with no roof from the spring to fall with his friends the peacocks. To Tanka's amazing surprise, she saw two peacocks scratching, digging and eating close to a circular cage. Tanka suddenly let out loud gobbles, yelps, and clucks, and dashed with her wings flapping, running quickly towards the cage. A sudden rush of excitement filled her. For that moment she forgot about her children.

The children were startled, but still ran quickly behind her; they were not sure what had happened. Kizi heard Tanka, but he thought he was dreaming. Kizi jumped up from behind the bushes where he was sitting and ran to the front of the cage. He saw Tanka. Tanka saw Kizi. She jumped up flapping her wings while she clucked and yelped. Kizi was gobbling and flapping his wings. The children joined in. Their reunion was a tremendous vibration of joy. From Tanka's great excitement she flew into the cage that Kizi was in. The children with excitement followed their mother flying into the cage to see their father.

For that morning and afternoon Tanka's and Kizi's reunion went from greeting each other to mating enjoyment. Tanka introduced Kizi to his three children. They were happy to be reunited with their father.

As the day went on, Tanka came to realize she and the children were in the cage, "Oh No," she said. She looked and saw two attendants feeding the deer in the caged pen next door to the cage she was in. "I must get out of here now," she said. She flew up and out of the cage. Her children followed her.

They had learned to follow the instincts and actions of their mother. They knew that there were very important lessons and outcomes for their mother's actions. Tanka knew she did not want to live in a cage with clipped wings.

As the day went by the peacocks flew back into the cage to eat. Tanka noticed their wings were not clipped and they seemed to like their caged home. She thought they liked being in the cage because the three of them, two males and one female, kept each other company, while Kizi was the only turkey.

Tanka felt Kizi had healed from his wounds and did not need to be in a cage, or as a matter of fact, did not have to be in the Environmental Center anymore. Tanka decided she was not going back into the cage. Tanka told Kizi she would return and went off to find food with her children.

At the end of that day, Tanka returned to Kizi's cage. She and the children slept in bushes close to the cage. From the bushes, she could see Kizi, who slept in the cage next to the fence so he could be as close to Tanka and the children as possible. Kizi now started to dream again of escaping. Tanka thought of ways to help Kizi escape.

Tanka woke up the next morning by the outside of Kizi's cage. She looked at Kizi and stretched, flapping her wings. Tanka noticed chipmunks running back and forth carrying acorns and leaves. Birds were flying up and down, back and forth. The sunlight streamed through the trees like water flowing in a steep brook. Humans were running, walking, and jogging, and cars drove by slowly.

Tanka became more aware of her environment. She also noticed trees swaying their branches back and forth from interaction with the wind, two cardinals hovering close to hibiscus plants and many geese and ducks. Men were cutting grass, park attendants were feeding animals in cages close by. Spring was in full bloom.

"This place is really busy," Tanka thought. She went to stand by Kizi, who was looking at her from inside the cage. The children were there, too. It was now seven days since Tanka was at the Environmental Center. She was having the urge to create a nest. She also remembered mating with Kizi for three nights since the first day she arrived.

The children were grown. While they visited with their father and searched for food to eat, Tanka was busy creating a nest in the bushes surrounded by huge grassy plants close to Kizi's cage. Tanka and the children were cautious not to be caught. When it was safe, the children would be out in the open, standing outside the cage while their father Kizi was in the cage.

Tanka laid five eggs after creating her nest. In between sitting on her eggs and finding food, she visited with Kizi. They would gaze into each other's eyes like star struck couples falling in love for the very first time. Tanka never forgot to take care of her eggs from predators and the weather. She would cover the eggs with leaves when she left, or have one of her children sit on the eggs, and sometimes the others would guard the eggs. Even with her extra protection of the eggs, two were eaten by a hungry raccoon and skunk.

Tanka's remaining eggs hatched. She had three children, three Jennies – female turkeys. When the children were old enough, Tanka brought them to show to Kizi by his cage.

On a bleak, rainy day, a hawk snatched one of Tanka's chicks, and one night, a fox sneaked up on them in the dark and grabbed one. Tanka now had only one chick left. She guarded this one with even more care. The Jenny grew very quickly over the next eighteen days. It was now summer. Tanka had taken the time to teach her chick all she should. Her baby turkey was now big and safer from predators.

Tanka was aware of the activities of the Environmental Center. She had gotten use to being there and was not so afraid of humans, although she was careful not to get caught. She made sure she did not go into the cage Kizi was in during the day. She slept with her children next to the fence most nights, with Kizi inside the cage sleeping close to Tanka and the children.

Daily they were separated by the fence, but they never let the fence get in the way of them being together as well as the love they had for each other. Rain or shine, Tanka was by Kizi's side, separated by the caged fence. She would sometimes wander around looking for food, teaching her children survival techniques. Tanka would bring Kizi bugs from her meal adventures. Kizi would give Tanka some of his food from his bowl inside his cage. They naturally found ways to connect, share, and express caring for each other in their situation.

Fall was arriving slowly; Tanka knew she had to create a nest for the winter. She and the children created a nest in a gathering of overlapping tree branches in the large deer-enclosed cage close to the cage Kizi was in. Tanka thought this was a safe place to nestle together with her children for the winter. The cage was large and surrounded by a fence. She and her children could fly in and out easily; and it was very close to Kizi's cage. Then one day she remembered that Kizi would be moved to another cage for the winter. She became sad again and wished that Kizi could escape.

The park attendants had not clipped Kizi's wings since the time she first came back to the center. Tanka and Kizi dreamed and wished for Kizi's escape. But they also knew that winter might not be the best time to escape. Plus it was getting close to the holiday and as long as they were in the Environmental Center, they would not end up being eaten.

"What a dilemma," they thought. Every day they made the most of each other's company. Tanka stayed most of the day by Kizi's cage wishing, dreaming, and praying for Kizi to be free.

"Freedom is free," Tanka thought sometimes. Repeating this gave her some comfort.

When it was time to transfer Kizi to the smaller enclosed cage for the winter, to Tanka and Kizi's great surprise the Environmental Center Manger had decided to let Kizi go free. Tanka, Kizi, and the children were so happy. The park manager took into consideration that Kizi had survived very well in the forest when he escaped; and that Tanka and the children were by Kizi's cage everyday from early spring to early winter. He guessed they were Kizi's family that was created when he had previously escaped. Plus, there was a new Jenny turkey. Kizi's wings had grown back so he could fly, and he was totally healed. Kizi was set free to live in freedom with his family.

Now Kizi, Tanka and the children were splendidly happy that their heart's desire had come true. Kizi had the choice of staying at the Center remaining free with his growing family, or of leaving with Tanka and the children to return to her parents in the forest. Wow, Tanka, Kizi and the children were so, so happy they thought that they were still daydreaming. They had to practice telling themselves that their dream and wish had come true. Tanka and Kizi decided to live in freedom at the Environmental Center.

That winter Tanka, Kizi and the children nestled together in the nest Tanka and the children had previously created. They lived happily in freedom at the center, where they were safe and had food.

Today, if you were to visit the Environmental Center, you would see Tanka and Kizi with their extended family creation living happily. Their turkey family has grown to fifteen turkeys. Bonded in love and teamwork, they eat, sleep, and play together as turkeys should. "Freedom is free, and love can sure find a way," said Tanka to Kizi. Kizi agreed and smiled.

Remember, dreams, prayers, and wishes can come true. And most of all always remember that love can find a way to improve any situation.

**The End**

# Chapter Three

# Ducky's Transformation

The sun rising to the east of the pond early in the morning created a shimmering glow across the green-colored pond by the nature center. Looking up into the sky almost to the west, the dim presence of the moon, almost invisible, represented the past.

Anna walked about twelve feet close to the root of a tree to present her usual morning offering: a gift of corn and flower seeds to feed the ducks, chipmunks, squirrels, and nature for accommodating her at the park on her usual early morning jog.

Many Canadian Geese and Mallard Ducks were swimming around the pond. Some played with one another; others seemed to be in disagreement about one thing or the other. Other Geese and Ducks were eating grass around the pond in a click, click rhythm as if keeping to the beat of the music created as their beaks passionately hit the blades of grass.

It's summer. The trees' branches were in their full essence filled with leaves that seemed to smile and wave. Branches were caressing and hugging. Overlapping branches created a cool, friendly, and shady atmosphere all over the park. The river to the east of the park rolled along, briskly bubbling over rocks and boulders, creating a feeling of peace and tranquility. Everything in the scenery seemed to fit like a completed puzzle.

The half-mile circular track around the pond was filled with people doing their early morning exercises. People were walking, jogging, running, biking, sitting on park benches having conversations with each other while they sipped beverages from their cups, listening to walkman, and talking on cell phones. The atmosphere was mixed and friendly.

Anna noticed that out on a very low tree branch, close to the water's edge was a strange looking duck sitting by itself. The duck was very beautiful and very different from the Canadian Geese and Mallard ducks.

The duck sitting alone had jet-black feathers with pink, purple, white, yellow and blue wings. It looked as if it was something from the fairy realm. It looked very majestic and divine. WOW.

"Where did this duck come from?" asked Anna. There were no others of its kind around. It was sitting there watching the other geese and ducks, but would not join them. Anna jogged around the track three times, but the duck still sat there by itself, alone. "Why is it not joining the others?" wondered Anna. It looked lonely but it might be ok. Anna left the park.

Each time Anna visited the park for her exercise she saw the duck sitting in a tree or standing in the bushes nearby where the other geese and ducks were eating. After seeing the duck behave in this manner for almost one month, Anna reflected on how much the duck reminded her of herself, observant, curious, alone and lonely sometimes, but also happy and content most times. "I guess it will be ok," she thought.

Every morning Anna was curious to see if the duck would be there the next day. Was it aware it was different? Could that be keeping it from mingling with the others? "Interesting," she thought. Would the other ducks not invite it into the flock? Did the other ducks and geese chase it away? Each morning Anna wished the duck would leave the branches or the bushes to join the other ducks.

One morning, to Anna's surprise, the duck was not sitting alone on the tree branch anymore. It was on the grass a little distance from the geese and ducks, eating grass by itself, sometimes sitting down. A man came over and took pictures of the colorful duck.

Anna felt relieved and happy. The duck seemed to be making a transition to not being alone anymore; moving from the comfort zone of the tree branch and bushes, to eating close by the other ducks and geese. Stepping out of its seemingly lonely confinements, and taking a risk to indirectly join the others. Two days later, it seemed as if the lonely duck was eating grass closer and closer to the others.

One beautiful sunny morning, to Anna's surprise, the beautiful lonely duck was eating grass with the other ducks. Without hesitation, the unique looking, colorful duck, while eating grass, magically found itself in the center of all the others. To Anna this was a great improvement for the duck's relationship skills. It totally merged with all the others in every way, except it stood out because of its outstanding colors.

Anna now thought maybe the duck, when she was first observing it, was trying to blend in, and taking time to observe and get to know its environment. The other geese and ducks did not seem to mind it being there. They all ate along merrily. It was happy and at home with the others. It ate with them for many mornings.

One morning about two month later, when Anna went on her usual morning jog, she did not see the colorful duck. Anna looked everywhere around the area of the pond. She did not see it. "I wonder where it went," thought Anna.

Ever since that day the colorful duck that chose not to be lonely anymore was nowhere around. Anna looked and looked where she usually saw it. The duck seemed to have left the park, or to have left this area of the park. To Anna, the duck flew away to an unknown destination leaving behind this beautiful story and reflections for her to review.

This duck really assisted and reinforced some of Anna's feelings about life. Sometimes, like this duck, we just have to choose to change our situation, or become open to change. Embrace fully what is desired the most. Believe in our desired intentions with all our hearts. Realize there are choices to transform one situation to another situation. Become aware that life is a story unfolding one step at a time. What we seek is always available, if only we can find the courage to open the doors of our eyes and heart to connect to it and take a chance.

If we can do these things and more, just like the beautiful colored duck, we can fly joyfully forward into the unknown, for the next part on our "Epic Journey of Life." And making friends can be useful.

**The End**

Chapter Four

# A Divine Partnership

Once upon a time on the planet Earth, Spirit, Mind and Body were traveling in a vehicle. This vehicle is within a magnificent force that was extremely mysterious. They came to the planet for a mysterious magical adventure. They traveled as explorers, and as clueless passengers, and companions. The mysterious adventure seemed to have no perceived beginning or end. So passengers Mind and Body cautiously sat back and began to read with Spirit the navigation maps to figure out what was going on.

Mind was cautious, curious, and impulsive all at the same time. Spirit, being the negotiator, was focused on the journey and the navigation system. Body was submissive and waited to be directed. Body sat quietly, close to Mind, observing what was happening. Spirit read the navigational map as giving them directions to go up the mountain, and Mind wanted to direct body to fool around, go down the mountain, and all around the place. Mind did not care about repetitiously ending up back in the same place and getting lost.

Mind thought transformation and new territories were no good; they lead to the unknown and unfamiliar territories, and maybe landscapes with too much light. Mind thought being asleep was cozy and productive. Taking leaps — forget it. Mind was afraid to fall. Mind was scared of heights and also of falling into a place it had no control.

Passenger Mind, as usual, liked being in charge, and being dominant, oftentimes ignoring Spirit when it did not want to hear what it was saying, influencing Body to go along with it. Passenger Mind also observed other vehicles going back and forth. Passenger Mind was especially friendly with the other minds in the other vehicles that were on the same wave length as it. This Mind turned a blind eye to the vehicles in which the minds seem to bond in harmony with spirit and body.

"I like being independent, important, and special," said Mind, "I do not like change, and I am focused on being in charge. I will do everything to keep things working my way."

When all three passengers worked together as a team, things were most productive, and went in favor of Spirit. But it was challenging to balance the relationship consistently amongst one another. To positively enjoy living they had to work together to really stay on the same wave-length and in the moment, all at the same time. This was the most difficult thing to do for passenger Mind. Mind oftentimes kept busy looking around for things to do, focusing in the past or planning for the future, ignoring Spirit and Body. Body trembled every time Mind did not stay connected to what Spirit was saying because Body always ended up agreeing with what Mind wanted to do, and then feeling the consequences.

Spirit was always sitting in the front seat using a navigational system that was invisible. Mind could only see Spirit's map clearly when it agreed with Spirit. Passenger Mind often would get irritated by this. Passengers Mind and Body often had a difficult time listening to Spirit. Mind consistently tried to get Body to not listen to Spirit. Body became worried by this because it knew this could have a lot of consequences. Body often pretended to be sleeping. They became aware that they had different roles to play in getting to the same destination that had no end and no beginning.

Mind and Body often thought someone was playing a trick on them, and Mind felt it must be in control to solve the problem. Spirit seemed to have most of the pieces to the puzzle and they had to co-operate with Spirit or things would get even more difficult, messy, and stuck, sometimes to the point that the vehicle fell into disrepair, and stopped moving. Mind likes to go fast liked a roller coaster, while Spirit likes to stop and smell the roses, and Body does just fine with not having to process any stress.

If Mind did not listen to Spirit, the vehicle would run out of fuel; Body developed a lot of pain and discomfort. Things would get pretty dark because sometimes Spirit would turn off the light. Body did not like the darkness. All the lights would go off in the vehicle; Spirit would become very irritated; and everyone would suffer.

Mind liked the darkness. It thought in the darkness Spirit could not see what it was doing, plus it could get to sleep more. Sometimes they became so lost, and the more they disagreed with passenger Spirit, the worse things would get. Spirit seems at all times to be most focused on what it wants to accomplish, and needs Mind and Body to co-operate. They became aware that in order for the most productive journey, it had to be a win-win situation, balanced in light, love and togetherness.

One day after Mind became very stuck and things could not get any darker, Mind surrendered to the fact that it must make the decision to free itself from its confining, controlling, manipulating, self-inflated box. Mind also figured out that changing its old ways would be extremely difficult, and staying in the moment to support Spirit and Body was even more difficult. Mind had to learn the seemingly impossible discipline of accepting Spirit as the Divine navigator and creator of Mind and Body. Mind reflected on the fact that if there is no Spirit, there can be no Mind or Body.

All of its life Mind tried to run away from the reality that Spirit was the one who manages the vehicle. That Spirit has the navigational map and the secret codes to read the map, and who creates from the source of the vehicle the light switch and fuel for the vehicle. At this time, Mind wanted to scream, but it could not speak because it was so stuck and could not make a sound out loud. Mind got so stressed out one day, it felt as if it were going to blow up or shut down. Mind took some time to do some more reflecting and came to a decision that at least it could try to become willing to transform.

With resistance, passenger Mind decided it would start to observe other minds in vehicles who worked as a team with Spirit and Body. Mind became very successful by becoming friendly with a mind from another vehicle. Mind's new friend's name was Awake. With Mind's new friend Awake's help, passenger Mind frequently communicated long distance, and received insights. Passenger Mind slowly began to understand what a productive process between Spirit and Body was like. Mind, without saying anything to Spirit, and Body, practiced in disguised and slow steps.

Spirit and Body noticed, but decided not to say anything to Mind about their experience and observation. Spirit and Body kept their fingers crossed and prayed Mind would continue to improve in the positive direction. Spirit and Body subliminally supported Mind's improvements.

Mind observed several things during its transformational journey, including: the mind that really thinks it knows everything is difficult to open. For every action there is an opposite reaction of the same action, called karma. Mind experienced that whether someone believes in karma or not, karma still happens. When someone focuses on resistance, resistance fights back. The Spirit is the principal navigator, connected to an even more powerful source. Passengers Spirit, Mind and Body, when working together as a team, are most successful. Staying in the present moment is important and productive. The wise ones hold nothing of Spirit or themselves back. Speaking and acting authentically from Spirit, the Mind connected to the heart. Mind without resistance can follow the positive energy with love and compassion through the Body. Mind, in harmony with Spirit and Body, can authentically express the energy of Spirit's intentions. There is no wrong or right when unconditional love is given and received. Experiences can create flawlessly paintings of colorful pictures of passionate dance and bliss. The human vehicle of Spirit, Mind and Body, saying one thing and intending another, can cause confusion. Minds that are cut off from their Spirit's feelings and emotions often express themselves from past and future experiences.

Mind's stress, fear, sadness, and disconcertment can cause depression, creating imbalances, shutdown, and division. Fresh ideas cannot be created. Living in the past and grasping for a future using the past as a map can be confusing, causing Mind unconsciously to be in denial of the present. The Mind cannot perceive that the present moment exists. Not realizing that the past and future are made up of the present moment, Mind can surely make itself suffer. Mind is a very important process that Spirit can use in the most productive way on this endless, timeless, and gateless journey.

After realizing and practicing the observations, Mind became more conscious. Mind realized, when communicating with other minds, two distinct energy forces were being expressed or not expressed. There is the Spirit trying to get through using a Mind that is stuck in the past, and not accomplishing its full potential. Sometimes the person feels like two entities, one whose physical body is trying to listen to his spirit, and at the same time listening to his mind. Both are usually in conflict. Body will usually seem to follow the Mind's path.

This is easier than changing what needs to be changed because Body cannot change without the Mind changing its negative habits. Body supports Mind by living the change. If Body does not live the change, then Mind has no other way to transform the energy of its old map. Mind likes to stay with what is familiar — not wanting to change or take a leap of faith. The more Mind tries to consume, the more tired and divided it becomes. It gets tired and caught up in fear.

A person cannot listen to his spirit if the mind does not choose to change being in charge, which expresses what we call an ego pattern. Ego is the self the mind creates to hide what is really going on. It can be difficult to understand this and change the old pattern of the mind. If a person transforms negative emotions associated with negative experiences and patterns of the past, he must then change the mind's map by living the intended positive change. Live the change so the mind can transform its old map to create the new map. Taking responsibility to choose new energy pathways, and letting go of the old pathways of people, places and things are of vital importance in changing the mind's map. One cannot seek healing and transformation and at the same time keep the old map.

All energies can be useful; yes, even negative ones. Negative energies can assist someone to the positive, but when the gate of positive is accessed, to get through the positive gate one must let go of the negative gate.

Passenger Mind also became aware some people hold onto others who are through the positive gate, not wanting to take full responsibility for their own healing or going through the positive gate themselves. Doing this takes away responsibility, choices, and empowerment, and can create what we call a co-dependant relationship. Co-dependant relationships will create negativity in everyone involved.

Without going anywhere you can know the whole world. You can know this through getting to know yourself. Without opening your eyes, you can know thyself. Mind saw the further away from itself it went into the past and future, the less it will really know. Usually, if someone looks around at the people, including friends in their life, they can see some reflection of themselves. The mind's mirror and everything else can be seen as a positive or negative reflection.

Passenger Mind observed that if someone is depressed, then the people in his life especially closest to him, and family members, can be a reflection of supporting his current emotional states. In this part of the planet, emotions seem to be an enemy. No one wants to get to know and express feelings.

Humans avoid the expression of feelings using medication, busyness techniques, and other deflecting devices. Mind observed that emotions are biofeedback of energy pulsing through every fiber of your being as feelings circulated, managed, and expressed by Mind. Negatively charged feelings, if left unattended, can cause big long-term negative problems. Positively charged feelings can create happiness, joy, and bliss, and can positively improve health and well-being.

Mind saw that some people's minds have a foolproof system of disconnecting, intersecting, manipulating, and controlling, and then a backup system. If the first system fails to counteract from coming into their conscious awareness any emotions that it is not familiar with, it does not realize that even if the awareness is not conscious, it still is a part of the energy system, mind and body, and is then mirrored in relationships and expressions. Mind became more awake to the conscious reality that it had a big responsibility.

At this point, without realizing how much transformation was occurring, Mind seemed to Spirit to have become a philosopher. Body was less stressed, and was filled with joy so that little by little the tensions in itself were transformed into peace. Mind kept at its practice transformation and learning. Frequently Mind would stop to rest more and more, meditating and reflecting.

Mind continued to learn that once energy is created or experienced it will not change and cannot be changed; it can only be transformed. So denial can be someone's biggest enemy. Because you have a foolproof denial system, and then ten more foolproof systems, does not mean that you are free from whatever you are trying to hide.

Wearing many masks, sweeping things under the rug, hiding behind camouflages, keeping busy, working too much, using mood altering drinks or foods, taking medications, and other things will create disguises, but it does not mean what you are hiding from has gone anywhere. It just means things are stored away until, at some point, everything breaks loose or becomes very stuck.

The person runs out of space to hide things, creating no ease. Doing these activities can create a more dark shadow self. Actually, the stronger the denial, the faster and more active the denial grows, causing bigger dysfunctions, less ease, expressed in mind, and body, recorded also in the Spirit's map and navigational system.

Mind also figured out that the human energy system is designed for two activities: healing and manifesting. At all times the spirit is seeking to heal that which is preventing it from manifesting its intention; and seeking to manifest that which it requires to heal damage and to positively transform to accomplish the reason why it created the mind and body. The true self, which is the spirit, gets to evolve and transform.

Wow, now Passenger Mind totally got what Spirit was saying and trying to teach it all along.

One day while they stopped under a tree to rest, Body was relaxing and having lunch, being tired and hungry. Mind asked of Spirit, "What is healing?"

Spirit said to Mind "Healing and manifesting are one and the same activity. On a physical plane, healing occurs when we channel, change, or rearrange matter. Healing allows us to manifest the desired positive improvement that is needed to make something positively better.

"Manifesting involves channeling, changing, or rearranging spiritual energy. No healing will occur if these two things do not happen. And for these two things to happen the choice must come from within the person who is seeking to heal. Healers do not heal; they assist the person who is choosing to heal to remove what is in the way and to give the resources so that the person seeking to heal, transform, and evolve can use the resources and opportunity to access the healer within themselves."

Spirit continued to tell Mind that every human's spirit came here to this planet equipped with everything they need for their journey, including whom they will find to assist them. This includes the person's parents and all their ancestors, intimate partners, husbands, wives, children and friends.

Parents and ancestors say a lot about what soul group people are currently in. They contain very important pieces of the puzzle of the journey. So everyone should get to know parents and ancestors as much as possible. They contain many keys to the chosen journey. Also reflect very compassionately on a chosen spouse, boyfriend, girlfriend, regular friends, people into which they come in contact. They are there to assist, if they are still around.

If someone does not fix what they need to fix within themself, the worst thing that could happen to magnify what needs to be fixed, is to end up choosing someone to live with as a mirror. When the purpose or karma of this person is over, their relationship with that person can change.

From what Passenger Spirit said, Mind realized there are no accidents in the Universe. Mind decided to stop and take a look at the map of itself, reflect, take an inventory of the people, places and things it currently comes in contact with. Mind realized that when it transforms, everything around transforms as well. Mind remembers everything is subject to transformation, and if the things, people, and places around are not changing, then Mind can be in a stagnant place.

Passenger Mind stopped to check to see if the stagnant place that it discovers itself in is where it chooses to be at the moment. "All energies can be useful for growth and transformation," said Mind.

Becoming more awakened, Mind discovered a new connection with Spirit. Mind realized that Spirit was a good friend and companion all along. Mind saw that Spirit glowed with loving kindness and compassion.

Mind was overcome with compassion and loving kindness as well. "Please tell me more," said Mind to Spirit.

"All right, as we go on the way, I will continue to talk," said Spirit. Body got up feeling pleasantly relaxed. Spirit, Mind, and Body as one vehicle continued up the path. Mind was mesmerized with Spirit and decided to source from Spirit from now on.

Mind decided that it would learn from its friend Spirit, and no longer choose to depend on other minds to learn. And that all three should connect as one in the vehicle like Spirit was saying all the time.

Spirit, Mind, and Body were now communicating bonded as one unit. Spirit continued to tell Mind, "Remember the future always contains the present moment as well as the past. So if you live in the moment, the future shows up on its own just by taking care of every present moment consistently and effortlessly. If you resist being in the present moment consciously or unconsciously, your resistance naturally fights back. Creating a continuous connection to the past can affect the present, which then creates a mirror into the future. Being in a cycle of skipping the present moments can create an imbalance in the mind, causing an imbalance in the chakras where the solar plexus chakra takes over the functioning of the heart chakra. The solar plexus chakra then teams up with the mind. The mind can then cut itself off from spirit, and heart. The mind becomes in charge, creating what we call the ego. The mind now reflects and creates the mirror of a self it is creating, separating from spirit, causing a split. An imbalance of the mind is the most complex imbalance to transform."

Mind said, "Spirit I feel that this was part of my issue before when we could not understand each other and see eye to eye." Body trembled to hear Mind finally admitting to this issue.

Body said to Spirit and Mind, "Hey I guess there is always room for improvement."

Spirit replied, "Yes indeed."

Spirit continued to tell Mind and Body the unpleasant stories that are left unresolved do not magically go away or get resolved by taking some magic pills, or someone waving a magic wand, by denial, or by projecting the problem on someone else. The person's mind must personally choose to connect to the story, change, transform the energy of the story, and change attitudes and lifestyle to transform the energy map in the mind. Then live the change they seek. Everything and everyone outside the Spirit, Mind, and Body are tools.

Spirit was recognized now by Mind and Body as a great teacher, so Spirit took the opportunity to continue since it had their undivided attention. "Getting assistance from professionals who can assist frequently is very important because someone's spirit, mind, and body cannot fix a problem from the same mindset that the problem was created, or the mindset of being in the eye of the energy that needs to be transformed. Once energy is created, it cannot be destroyed, it has to be transformed. Anything outside the individual is a tool for change and transformation, including all the healing arts."

Mind at this time told Spirit and Body what it did to improve to where he was at the moment. They found Mind's story and journey very interesting. Spirit noted, "A great mind is a terrible thing to waste. Good that you seek help outside yourself; not every mind has this ability. We are all now very happy Mind that you did take responsibility to do something about your situation."

Communicating to Mind and Body, Spirit continued like a freight train going up a hill. "Continuously individuals keep tripping over themselves, the mind and body, going back repetitively through the same unproductive energy pathways, and spirit has to tag along. Spirit is often wondering what to do to change the situation or to focus on being optimistic that things will one day change. If this continues to happen frequently, the person should seek some neutral assistance. Someone cannot fix a problem from the same place they created it. Most times a spouse, who should be the closest independent person to someone, will mirror what should be fixed in the person. Sometimes this is scary to own, recognize, or see. If someone is disconnected from love, then most times both persons are disconnected from love in some way."

Spirit said to Mind and Body: "Love is energy. Love is not an action or a feeling. Actions and feelings can express the energy of love, and also actions and feelings can create the energy of fear. Light/love, fear/darkness are a pair, like the foot in front and the foot behind in walking. Each has its own intrinsic value and is related to everything else in function and position. But know that the energy of love, through actions and feelings, productively builds up; it does not break things down. Fear breaks things down or creates dis-function, and sadness, giving something or someone the opportunity to restart or begin anew. So if someone is in a relationship with someone or something and calls it love, then it should be creating productive, functional, joyful results."

Mind said to Spirit and Body: "So love creates positive light, fear creates negative darkness. So I should begin to recognize when I am in love, or in fear, and call it by its true name. This responsible choice can be priceless and very useful if I am on the path to really healing, transforming and growing. I should remember the energy of fear breaks things down and the energy of love builds things up. Both can be useful and they work together as mates."

Again Mind very reflectively asked of Passenger Spirit, "So when I see you glowing is it because you are connected to, and channeling the energy of love?"

"Yes. It also means that the vehicle of Mind, Body and Spirit are connected in harmony to the magnificent Positive Life Force in the Universe that creates all things," said Spirit.

Body was enjoying this new creation of unity and love among all three of them. Body hummed a tune as it peacefully continued the now transformative adventure of Spirit, Mind and Body.

Body said to Spirit and Mind, "So as we flow in the springs, rivers, and oceans of life, we should remember to give attention consciously to what is happening unconsciously. These two functions also work as mates. Try to improve mind's quality by bringing the unconscious to the conscious present moment awareness, to be attended to. The energy that is created on the path of the waters of life's journey will flow to the ocean of all life and have an effect on life, and also on all living things. We are all connected, and interdependent. We are creators of our life experiences and the Universe. Mind and Body are very important on the journey of Spirit having a human experience. Everything is energy. Energy is everything. Bring mind's awareness to spirit's awareness and bring to body the messages of what to create for productively improving the journey. And the most important thing is to enjoy whatever you are experiencing, creating, or have created."

"Wow, very interesting. We now understand even more," said Mind and Body in unison.

The vehicle stopped at a crossroad. Passengers Mind and Body came out of the back of the vehicle and joined Spirit in the front of the vehicle. Passenger Mind sat in the middle. Passenger Body breathed a sigh of relief.

Spirit and Body said, "Thank you" to Mind. Mind replied, "You are welcome."

Mind promised to work with Spirit and Body as a team, filtering to the Body whatever energy and information Spirit wanted to accomplish. Mind finally became aware of how it could practice every minute, productively staying awake, in the moment; how it could accomplish real positive progress, and learn how to understand its self worth and purpose. Mind saw how it could blend effortlessly into Spirit, giving up control, becoming peaceful, quiet, calm, and positively productive, and blending into Spirit, achieving the essence of no mind.

Mind realized at a deeper level that having nothing to do and no place to be, just enjoying the gateless, timeless adventure of

Spirit's mission, was effortless and fun. Doing this, Mind got to see it was getting more than it could ever imagine. Mind saw it was getting its way with not doing, but just being. Mind shouted, "This is magical!"

With this awareness, Mind smiled. For the first time it could see the journey effortlessly. Mind saw how becoming interdependent, and less judgmental and rebellious, can be more productive. With this awareness Mind relaxed and became peaceful and content. Peacefully they grew happily together as they continued the endless mysterious adventure of energy and information, evolving endlessly as they journeyed together in their vehicle of love and light.

At this point, overhead the stars were smiling and winking, and the full moon was beaming. The sky was raining down and around darkness. They realized that it was night. They were all so tired. Spirit pulled the vehicle over into a rest stop and they all fell asleep within minutes.

Spirit, Mind, and Body working together in balanced partnership can be transformative, productive, peaceful, joyful and harmonious. Spirit was now completely at peace that its dream had come true. Now it could effortlessly continue on the path and mission of improving the gateless and timeless infinite vehicle of Source Energy, Spirit, Mind, and Body.

**The End**

## Chapter Five

# The Three
# Tree Friends

A t this time, at a place far, far away and deep in the inner realm lives Leila. Growing up Leila lived with her parents and grandparents and little brother Ned. Her little brother Ned was three years old and liked to follow Leila wherever and whenever he possibly could. The place where they lived was very magical. It was a huge property, where nature seemed so alive.

The green landscape was as green as dark emeralds, with flowers of many kinds and colors that had the brightest and sharpest shades of colors that just seemed to shine, sparkle and smile. A dancing brook babbled, shimmered and rolled through the property. The animals from the bushes would gather by the brook for a friendship celebration, to rest, and to play. The trees would seem to communicate in whispers of different tones to one another. During the day trees stood like majestic thrones viewing the landscape and enjoyed swaying in the wind. The trees seemed to have eyes that stared at you curiously. If you can visibly see a tree's many eyes, then you can sense and see its spirit, too. At night the spirit of the trees would wander around exploring. When someone would encounter a tree spirit at night, the tree's spirit would avoid the person or go right through their body.

Bees were busily taking nectar from flowers. The bees seemed so excited and intoxicated their absorption of nectar was like a drunken exotic dance from flower to flower, and from blossom to blossom. The wind whispered. The wind, swimming all around, seemed to caress, dip, and dive. Really, if your heart and mind were quiet, you could hear the conversational exchange amongst the things in nature at this magical place.

Birds chirped harmonious tunes, flying from place to place, or hopping around, bobbing up and down. Everything seemed to exist in peace, fun, and musical harmony. If you were to visit this place, you would feel the invisible presence of life-force energy and magical presence that seemed unexplainable. Out of the corner of your eyes you might catch a quick movement of some kind, but physically not see anything.

The stones would also seem to come alive and speak in low grumbling tones. Mother Nature was enjoying herself in each moment, infinite, simple and so profound. This place was unbelievably interesting to Leila because she could experience what was happening. Leila so far has never talked to anyone about what she was experiencing.

All of these magical moments were Leila's big secret. Leila's brother in his own way seemed to know what was going on. He seemed to be in tune with it all. Leila said nothing to him; he said nothing to Leila. They said nothing to their parents.

To them the experiences were normal, but in a way not really because their parents or grandparents never discussed what they were experiencing with them.

Ned loved to pretend he was a bird flying. He would run and glide around with his arms stretched out to his side. When the animals gathered by the brook, Ned was there talking to them, and they seemed to talk back to him. Sometimes Leila was at the brook as well, doing the same thing. Ned also loved to draw; he seemed to have a creative imagination that surpassed normal. His drawings and paintings seem to come alive. There was an energy that brought his pictures to life. Sometimes he talked to the picture he was drawing as if the drawing was really alive. Ned was a fascinating kid.

Leila's most favorite thing to do was to hangout in the woods with her three tree friends, to tell stories, to ask questions and to write in her book. She would write short stories. Leila had quite a collection of stories that she kept in a wooden box under her bed against the wall. These stories were her treasure and the box was her treasure chest.

Leila's three tree friends were pine, flowering plum and bamboo. These three trees seemingly had spirits as wise and as ancient as the planet. When Leila asked questions or had general conversations with these trees, their communication back and forth and amongst all of them was as if communicating with humans. They helped Leila write stories and see things from a very unique perspective. Sometimes they each helped her with her homework.

Leila's relationships with these trees were normal to her. She was a young child of about two years old when she first discovered these trees. One day she wandered away from a family party that was being held outside close to the rambling brook. Trying to get onto a swing tied to the flowering plum tree, she felt that something was helping her. At such a young age she was aware and accepted that this invisible presence was normal. To Leila, her relationship with the trees was normal as normal could be.

One day Leila became sick with the flu. The doctor told her parents that she should stay warm, and rest in bed until her fever and flu symptoms had improved. After doing this for five days, although Leila's flu symptoms had decreased, she was not feeling much improvement. She also had felt lonely and missed her tree friends, and melancholy seemed to fill her and her room. On the sixth day Leila told her mother she needed some fresh air and wanted to go outside to visit her tree friends. Leila's mother agreed. Off Leila went skipping, and humming. She brought her notebook with her.

On her way to the very shady and calm cluster of bamboo, pine and flowering plum trees, she saw her brother Ned at his favorite place by the brook. Making paper boats, Ned was sailing them into the shallow brook. "Hi Leila, can I come with you?" Ned asked.

"No, not today," replied Leila, skipping and hopping as she hurried to get to her tree friends.

When Leila arrived, her tree friends were happy to see her. For the first time the pine tree spirit told her that their spirit could leave the tree and that they came to visit her in her room. Then all three tree spirits showed Leila an example. Their spirits left the tree and came over to where Leila was standing. She felt a cool breeze all around her as they came towards her. She also saw invisible footprint-like impressions on the grass and leaves that were on the ground. Leila stood in amazement and laughed.

"Wow, who, what, how, do you all do this!" Leila said shouting with surprise. Pine tree spirit told her to lie on the carriage swing that seated three people. This swing was tied to the flowering plum.

An old swing was built and tied up in strong branches of the plum tree by her father and grandfather many years ago. Leila walked slowly over to the swing and lay down with her notebook under her head. She felt a sudden sleepiness. As she laid there, the three tree spirits of pine, plum, and bamboo trees gathered around her. Leila suddenly, as if by divine intervention, fell into a deep, deep sleep.

With the help of Mother Nature's energy, and consciously being in the tree spirits elements, a generous source of life-force energy was directed to Leila and she received it with open heartedness. She slept for about three hours.

"Wake up, wake up," Leila's mother Doris said as she shook her. "I was wondering where you were, it is dinner time. Come on let's go inside for dinner."

Leila slowly opened her eyes and she saw everything so clearly. She noticed as well that her flu symptoms and cold were gone. They magically left and more over, she felt cool and revitalized. Her whole body felt like new. Leila looked around her quickly. She said, "Mom go on in, I will be there in five minutes."

"Alright", her mother said and left.

Leila went over to each one of her tree friends and said, "Thank you," as she put her hands together and gave a graceful bow to each one and gave them a hug. "I will see you tomorrow," she said to them.

Leila ran towards her home. When she arrived, everyone was seated at the dinner table. She washed her hands and sat in her seat. Her father Daniel said, "Leila you look great and your cheeks are light pink, are you feeling better?"

"Yes, oh yes," Leila replied. Then she was silent again. She sat quietly. She felt as if she was dreaming. At dinner she was actually daydreaming about the events of the afternoon with her tree friends. Leila replayed the events over and over in a daydream-like state. Leila was brought back to consciousness when her father touched her on her arm and asked her if she was ok, because she was so quiet and seemed to be in another place. She told him she was all right. At that point Leila told everyone she was feeling great, better than she has ever felt, renewed, with all her flu symptoms including the fever, gone as if eliminated by magic.

"Wow!" everyone said simultaneously in unison.

They were surprised. After dinner, Leila helped with cleaning up the table and assisted her mother to wash and dry the dirty dishes, utensils, pots and pans. Grandma and Grandpa had gone outside to sit on the porch where they held hands and talked until they were ready to sleep. Leila's father had taken her brother Ned upstairs to give him a bath and get him ready for bed, read him a story, and put him to bed for the night.

After Leila and her mother Doris had finished with the dinner clean up, her mother said, "Leila, I will tell you starting tomorrow after school the stories of the trees. There are three trees that are very special to our family on the property. I see that you have already discovered them and made them your friends. I noticed that where they are is your most favorite place. I see you there writing, sitting in the swing, and also talking to them."

Leila was very surprised about what her mother had said. Leila replied, "Mama what about the trees, tell me now." Her mom told her to go upstairs and get ready for bed it was too late to start the story. It was bedtime.

"Tomorrow we will begin the story of our favorite trees," said Doris.

Leila went to get ready for bed. She could not wait to hear the story. After the day's events, Leila was ready for a long, restful night's sleep. For the first time in six days she felt completely well, excited, and at the same time, blissfully sleepy. After lying in her bed for about three minutes, Leila fell fast asleep.

Knock, knock, knock — there was a loud knock on Leila's door. She had overslept. "Wake up Leila. Get dressed quickly or you will be late for classes," said her father Daniel.

"Wow!" Leila said jumping up. "I am coming," said Leila. She had such a restful sleep; she wished she could continue to sleep. She could smell breakfast streaming through the door like mist. She also could hear her mother as usual humming a tune as she got breakfast on the table, and lunches organized. Leila was nine years old when she attended school three times a week from 8:30 in the morning to 1:30 in the afternoon.

Life in the inner realm was simple and going to school at Leila's age was a part-time activity. The people of the inner realm felt life was a mixture of different kinds of experiences that were enjoyable and peaceful.

Today was a school day for Leila. She enjoyed her breakfast and off to school she went. After school, Leila did her chores. She visited her three tree friends pine, bamboo and flowering plum. Leila told them what her mother had said about telling her the story of the ancestor's tree relationship. The trees smiled and waved their branches.

The tree spirit knew when Leila was of age her mother would give her the rites of passage of the three tree stories. Leila left her tree friends and went home to help her parents prepare supper. They ate. After dinner when the kitchen was cleaned up and all were ready for bed, Ned was read a story, and tucked into bed by his father. Leila sat in her room with her mother to begin the story of the trees.

Leila's mother began the story told to her by her parents, who received the transmission of the tree story passed down generation after generation. As the story goes: Long, long ago when the inner realm was young, and humans had not yet arrived in the inner realm, the pine, bamboo and flowering plum tree spirits came to the inner realm, liked it and decided to stay. Being in the inner realm gave the trees opportunity to see and experience everything as a mirror of themselves. For the trees, it is as if looking into a mirror.

The trees loved the planet, the atmosphere, the earth, rain, sun, moon, stars, air, clouds, and all the other things of the inner realm so very much that they decided to stay till this day. Humans came many, many hundreds of years later. Glazed into the innocence of trust, the trees, plants, nature spirits, birds and other animals felt safe and peaceful living in peace and harmony.

Few humans came at first. These few humans wandered around peacefully enjoying themselves. The humans also lived in harmony with everything, enjoying their daily adventures. Everything: trees, animals, plants, humans and their children supported one another living curiously and fearlessly.

"So Leila, yes, trees are like people. They have a spirit. Trees have feelings and magical healing powers. Treat them with respect and love and they will help you in a friendly, nourishing way. But just like humans, some tree spirits can be unfriendly, mean, and just want to be left alone."

Mother Doris continued, yawning and seeming tired. Sleepily she went on: Trees are very important to all of life in the inner realm. They clean the atmosphere, recycle toxic gasses back into the atmosphere as clean gasses for all living things to live and function; they pull water down into the earth to feed the earth, the life forms within the earth and then in turn feed themselves. Trees release water through their leaves and branches to moisten the air and to assist with the cycles of rain, weather and climate. The leaves of the trees fall off back to the earth to feed it and to create more expansion of earth. Out of the earth all resources are created. Trees create within their trunk, roots, and branches a home for many rodents, insects and other animals, including humans. Trees are transformed into lumber, which provides natural building resources to create many things. Paper comes from trees. Food comes from trees. Without trees, all of life would be different. The wisdom of the planet, Universe, and all living things are in the spirit of trees.

At this point both Leila and her mother were beyond staying awake. Both of them, at this point, desperately needed to sleep. "I will continue tomorrow after dinner," said Leila's mother.

Leila kissed her mother goodnight. "Thank you mama," Leila said as she crept into bed like a spider and snuggled into the cozy web of her sheets. Within three minutes Leila was fast asleep like a tired owl that had not slept for weeks.

On night number two, Leila's mother, began: On this property my great, great grandfather planted the pine, bamboo and flowering plum tree. As time went on and as the family came and went, we made it a special and important tradition to pass down from generation to generation the transmission of our story of the three special trees: pine, bamboo and flowering plum. We feel that in doing so the trees continue to regenerate and duplicate their lifespan. They are respectfully honored and supported to begin anew, and continuing until this day.

She continued her story: Pine trees are the great evergreen. They are one of the inner realm's greatest and most beloved trees. Their beauty is timeless and their endurance goes from season to season, territory to territory and environment to environment. They can withstand the different climates and weather, and during snowy season give off a reassuring presence of greenery blanketed by snow, letting life remember that under the blanket of winter's snow, life still exists with a pleasant green glow. During the Christmas holiday, pine trees are used to make wreathes, garlands, and Christmas trees that symbolically represent joy, sharing, caring, renewed life, rebirth, long life, wisdom and relaxation.

There are about one hundred and twenty-five species of pine trees found in the inner realm. Pinecones are used for craftwork, and pine oil can be used to assist the symptom of stress. Pine needles, sap, bark, and nuts were used by her grandfather for medicinal purposes. Doris also said her father told her the pine trees were viewed by him to represent, honor, strength, long life, wisdom, integrity, heaven, earth, success and abundance.

As long as the pine trees were around, my parents and other ancestors were content. The pine tree is sacred. It holds the ancient story of life's creation. The spirit of the tree keeps alive the physical tree you see. Sometimes the spirit of the pine tree is renewed to continue the life of the physical tree. The one big pine tree you see over where the bees are busy taking nectar from the blossom of the sage bush, and where sometimes the fairies are sitting on the huge peppermint and lavender flowers, created all the other pine trees on the property.

When my great, great grandfather planted the first pine, bamboo, and flowering plum trees, he knew that they were the three tree friends of winter. They kept each other company during the winter months. The pine tree stays evergreen and strong, motivating all other life forms up and throughout the journey of winter and the chilling blanket of winter's blistering snowy frost.

Doris noticed Leila had started to fall asleep. She could hardly keep her eyes open. "Time to go to sleep. We will continue after dinner tomorrow," said Doris. Leila again went to sleep peacefully; this time she fell asleep on the floor of her room. Her mother lifted her and placed her into her bed. She covered her, turned off the light, and slowly closed the door. Everyone else had gone to sleep. Doris took a warm shower and quietly went to bed next to her husband Daniel.

The satisfaction, companionship and bond grew within Leila for her mother, and the trees, as her mother continued the journey of the story. Leila was becoming more and more aware of the sacredness and importance of the trees. Now when Leila visited the trees, she would share some of the story with them.

On the third night, Doris told Leila the story of the bamboo tree. "The spirit of the bamboo tree," she said, "is very mysterious, clever, abundant, affluent, flexible, looks weak but is very strong, humble, willing, rejuvenating, and continuously practicing emptiness. This is why bamboo is hollow within. The bamboo is also committed to continuous growth. This is why when bamboo grows it continues to expand its growth in numbers, popping up and out of the earth like soft thorns. Last but not least, the bamboo represents simplicity. Bamboo simply and abundantly expands it root system, creating many more bamboo shoots and tree system."

Doris said to Leila, "My father told me his father practiced diligently the seven principles of the bamboo tree. His father taught him, he taught me, and now I will tell you of these principles that you will practice in your chosen way.

"Principle number one: Bend as many times as you choose to. Bend in any directions you choose to. When you bend, hold the awareness of not breaking. This will help you to be flexible yet firmly rooted. Bend, but try to avoid breaking. Bamboo sways back and forth with even the slightest breeze. Their physical structure is hard and solid and yet they sway so effortlessly while staying very rooted into the earth. Even the youngest of bamboo trees know this. They learn this from before they are born.

"Shooting up from within the earth, the roots of older bamboo give birth from within to new shoots of bamboo, encrusted and protected by a shell-like casing. Swaying bamboo is solid even though they move with the wind. Even after the strongest wind has visited the bamboo, the bamboo tree stands tall, green and elegant. The bamboo goes with the natural flow of things effortlessly continuing the dance and adventures of life.

"Principle two of the bamboo is learning that sometimes things do not look like they seem. Some things that look weak can be very strong. Bamboo shoots look slender, weak, and fragile but they can endure extreme weather and climate conditions. During a storm, bamboo can withhold strong winds. Bamboo trees are sometimes the only ones left standing after a storm.

"Bamboo trees usually stay healthy. When bamboo plants get old and their life span naturally have come to an end, they turn brown, decay, and effortlessly fall to the ground. The old saying goes, 'Do not judge a book by its cover. And be careful to not underestimate who someone is by only using what you physically see."

"Leila, your real strength is channeled from within the empty cores of the five pillars of your being," said Doris.

"What are the five pillars of a Human Being?" Leila asked her mother.

Doris said, "They are your physical, emotional, mental, spiritual and the connection to the higher source know as the creator, God, Universe, or whatever anyone's connection is to a higher power." It was time for bed and Leila and her mother took a shower and retired for a well-needed sleep.

On the fourth night after dinner Doris continued. "Principle number three is being as ready as you can be to experience whatever life brings your way, like bamboo that is always ready without forcing or showing off. Practice with diligence being the best and doing the best to positively improve whatever you choose to do daily. Through continuous and consistent practice you can naturally develop readiness.

"Principle number four: Cultivate and practice the ability to reset and come back to a balance and functioning place. If you ever experience difficult situations, make sure that you are learning the lessons of the experience. Ask for help and assistance if you need to regain balance and positive function.

"Principle number five is cultivating and practicing beginners mind; seeing from the eyes of a child, remaining teachable, empty, quiet, inquisitive minded, positively explore and learn new things. Within emptiness is true wisdom. The bamboo finds wisdom within the emptiness of the hollowness within. Someone who thinks and feels they know everything has no room to learn and explore new things to awaken to more of their talents and wisdom. The more a cup is empty, the more room it has to be refilled and refilled. There is wisdom in the emptiness of the bamboo."

Doris stopped at this point for the night. Leila had not completed her home–work and it was already late. "Finish your homework for school," said Doris. "I am going to check on Ned and read him a story," she continued as she left Leila's room. Doris husband's Daniel had prepared Ned for bed. Ned was playing with his airplanes as he waited for his mother.

On the fifth day, Doris continued with principle six of the bamboo tree. It was still the afternoon. She had begun her story with Leila right after she had returned from school. Leila's grandparents were making supper that day. It was Friday.

"Principle number six: Always know that you have infinite potential to grow. Never give up. The bamboo tree is one of the fastest growing plants in the inner realm. Commit to continuous, positive, and productive growth.

"Principle number seven of the bamboo lesson is find simple but very constructive ways to create all the things you like as you experience life. Stay consciously connected to each step so you stay connected to the wisdom within each step. Each step of everything you create is like a sacred building block that contains strength in the unspeakable language of fearless, confident simplicity. The simple basic foundation of life is simplicity. Bamboo finds many simple ways to express its usefulness and simple form. For example, bamboo can be used to create a flute, a strong fence, a house, mats, and beds. Bamboo can be used to make so many useful and constructive things.

"From now on when you visit the bamboo tree, observe and see for yourself as you grow the seven principles of the bamboo tree. Ask the bamboo tree spirit to show you these principles," Doris told Leila.

"Mama I am tired and it is sunny outside. I would like to go visit the trees now, and before dinner I will take a short nap in the swing tied to the plum tree," said Leila. "Ok," mama Doris said.

It was Friday and traditionally in their home everyone after dinner gets to spend quiet time individually doing something they choose and love to do. Doris told Leila that she would continue the story of the trees the next morning after breakfast.

Saturday came and it was time to begin the story of the flowering plum tree. But first, the whole family had breakfast together, and afterward they did their chores. Everyone working together, they cleaned up the kitchen and the whole house. Each child was responsible for cleaning up his or her room, and bringing the dirty laundry down to the laundry room for the grandparents to do the laundry. Father Daniel cleaned up the kitchen and the living room, and mother Doris cleaned her bedroom, the bathrooms, and brought some dirty clothes to the laundry room. Her grandparents had cleaned their own room before going down to do their laundry chores.

When all the chores were completed Leila and her mother would spend time together; and Ned would go to his usual spot by the babbling brook to play until his father was ready to take him fishing. Daniel would first go into town to do food shopping before going fishing. After the shopping he would take Ned with him to go fishing by the river close to their home. After completing the laundry her grandparents would go for an afternoon walk together and to visit their friends along the way.

"Wow! Mama the journey of the tree is so magically interesting. I never dreamed this experience was coming," said Leila to her mother.

"Yes there is more to life than you can ever dream and when the time is right things usually come into bloom and creation." replied mama Doris.

"Wait Mama, I would like to get some lemonade before you continue with the legend of the flowering plum tree. Would you like some too, Mama?" asked Leila.

"Yes, no ice for me," replied her mother. Leila skipped dragging her feet through the grass and she also hummed a tune as she went to get two glasses of lemonade.

Leila came back. She sat on the swing tied to the flowering plum tree. Her mother sat on a bench close by. The tree spirits and nature spirits gathered around them curiously, sharing their energy vibrations. Butterflies, bees, and wasps went busily from flower to flower, and herbs blossom. When Leila came back with the glasses of lemonade, her mother began the story.

"There are many ancient stories surrounding the flowering plum tree. The five petals symbolically represent the five pillars of all living things – source of God – spirit– mental – emotional – physical. Also the five senses of seeing, smelling, hearing, tasting, feeling, the five elements of earth, water, fire, air, spirit, and the five Chinese blessings of old age, wealth, health, love of virtue, and a natural death.

"The flowering plum tree would blossom during the winter, bringing pleasant joyful atmosphere to the other trees and life in general. For all these reasons, the three trees were planted close to each other, and additional essence of togetherness, friendship, and positive harmonious relationships surround these magnificent trees.

"The flowering plum is also said to represent perseverance and purity because it is the first flower to appear in early spring in some countries and blossoms when there is still snow on the ground. Also, because it is the first tree flower to bloom during winter, it symbolizes vitality and vigor of nature, smiling even during winter's chilly embrace. A part of the tree's essence is said to be protective when planted in a northeastern section of a property.

Some people believe the plums from the flowering plum tree can be eaten to enhance the essence of good fortune. Doris said her parents taught her how to use the plums in many ways. For example, to make plum pudding, juice, bread, liquor, cakes, wine, pickled plum, stewed plum with different meats and rice, plum as a snack, in salads, soups and sometimes leaving very ripe plums on the ground to rot and become fertilizer to nourish the earth, plum tree, and the other plants around. Her parents told her plums can be smoked and used to cleanse the stomach and colon free of parasites, stop the symptom of ulcers, and to strengthen the heart and digestive system."

"This completes all I have to share with you about the wisdom and wealth of the three tree friends of winter," Doris said to Leila.

"They are my three tree friends, too," said Leila.

Leila in many ways felt blessed by the information, wisdom, teachings, and beauty of her mother's stories. She would always treasure their valuable lessons, sacredness, and wealth of wisdom. She found it very interesting and amazing that she naturally became friendly with the trees on her own just like her mother and other ancestors did in the past.

As Leila continued to grow, when the time was right, her mother expanded on her natural awareness and relationship with the trees. She also showed and shared with Leila the ancestors' traditional plum recipes for food and health remedies.

As Ned grew he too, naturally gravitated to spending more time with her by the trees. He also was given the transmission and stories of the three tree friends. For Ned, as well, the rights of passage of the three tree friends were performed by his mother Doris. She truly enjoyed passing on the awareness of the trees' importance. Their ancestors' traditional story of the trees continued very smoothly with Ned, being the last child to receive the transmission of the stories from their mother.

In the present time in the inner realm, the tradition of the three tree friends stories continues without exception. This tradition, the family feels, is a part of their mystical secret success to experiencing positive health, well-being, success, long life, abundance, affluence, strength, unity, healthy relationships, among other things.

The tradition continues. Leila's grandparents and parents lived a long, healthy life. Leila and her brother Ned continued the transmission of the three tree friends stories with their families. The interesting and magical thing is that their children, naturally on their own, discovered the three tree friends when it was time. The parents and trees with natural delight continue their lessons, and teachings.

Today, if you were to visit them in the inner realms in middle earth, you will see the three tree friends, Leila, her husband and three children, Ned and his wife and their five children. They all live on this property in the inner realm. Go visit them and you will see and learn. Or you can create your own relationship with trees you like. You might find this magical and interesting.

**The End**

*Chapter Six*

# *Introduction to the Seven Major Chakras*

*I* grew up from birth with my grandmother in a small village in Montego Bay, Jamaica, West Indies. We lived simply with the assistance of the spirit, air, earth, fire, water, the sun and the moon. People could tell by the energy in the air what the weather would be. In mother earth we planted the vegetables and other food we ate. The animals were also fed by the grass and plants from the earth. The foundation of our kitchen floor was earth. For cooking we used dry wood for fire, with large stones to secure the wood. Crisp and sparkling water flowed from numerous rivers, streams and small brooks. I had to walk about three miles every day to get water for our personal use. I carried this water home balanced on my head in a large bucket. Water splashed down, sometimes when I walked. I loved doing this, it felt refreshing. I had to make more than one trip.

We got up when the sun starts to rise. The sun was one of the main ingredients for us, the plants, and everything that grew. The sun was one of our main energy suppliers. We did not have electricity or plumbing in the village. We went to the bed when the moon came, because the sun had to go. They watched over us like father (masculine) and mother (feminine); taking turns. There were no medical doctors, medical or mental health facilities.

Looking back I can see how everything was in peace, harmony, happiness and love - (in balance). The Chakras of the people and the environment were in harmony and balance with each other.

Everything was effortless. With this foundation in my earlier life my chakras are secure. My chakras in and outside of my body assist me in flowing between the banks of pleasure and pain and not getting stuck in either. I am here to assist.

There are a lot of other books explaining the chakras and how they function. This awareness is intended to start you on your journey back to yourself. Reminding you of one of the important part of how your energy system functions. It is like the key opening the door back to you. After opening your door, you will journey on to understand who you really are, from other great teachers, through their books. You will get to see we are not only human; we are spiritual beings having a human experience. We are a bundle of energy, matter, and information. The chakras assist us in our inner and outer world. They also assist us in growing spiritually through pain and pleasure. I hope the information in this book will serve as an awakening for your spiritual, personal development and self awareness. Your foundation is like a rainbow.

Chakra is a Sanskrit term meaning "wheel of light." There are seven major in body chakras. The chakras are spinning vortexes of subtle energy located along the spine, from the end of the trunk of your body to the top of your head. As they spin they can radiate different spectrums of light and color. The seven chakras are energy centers, doors and transformers that receive, distribute, store, and release energy in and out of the body. Not visible to the usual sight they look like conical funnels. The first six, starting from the end of the spine is two sided, with one side spinning out the front and the other out the back. The chakra which vibrates from the crown is also two sided. One side is less open to view because it opens into a higher dimension than the others. Chakras regulate, maintain, and manage the physical, emotional, mental, and spiritual aspects of our being on the physical level. Some of their other functions are:-

+ Connecting life to the multidimensional universe
+ Record, store, regulate and communicate energy vibrations within you and outside of you; interacting with all other life in the Universe.

The energy centers must all be open and in balance to experience wholeness. Most of us react to challenging situations in our lives with anger, insecurity, or fear, never realizing that we create what we experience. You may think that difficult situations and emotions experienced are caused by other people or random events. It is your imbalance depending on how your energy centers are functioning, that creates the situations that interfere with your sense of well-being and contentment. Life is energy (Chi). Your energy positive or negative affects all your experiences. The chakras are about energy and balance. Their balance or imbalance can affect your life positively or negatively. There are certain techniques that can be incorporated into your daily lives to assist in increasing or decreasing the quality of energy your chakras distribute. These techniques include Reiki, Yoga, Meditation, Qigong, Tai Chi, being mindful, practicing unconditional love and not having clutter. You are the mirror of your perception; your body and life reflects back to you what it sees.

Below is the order of the chakra from crown (center top of the head) to the root at end of tail bone, which includes sexual organs, hips, legs, and feet.

+ Crown **#7**
+ Third Eye **#6**
+ Throat **#5**
+ Heart **#4**
+ Solar Plexus **#3**
+ Sacral (two inches below belly button **#2**
+ Root (end of tail bone, sexual organs, hips, legs, feet) **#1**

# First Chakra
# Element: Earth

Location: Base of the tailbone -
Seat of Kundalini energy.
Color: Red
Vibration: Urge for Survival & Individuality

This is the root of your being and the deepest connection to your body and earth. It is the prime mover behind the so called fight-or-flight response. If a person experience trauma of any kind, this can affect this energy center in a negative way. Located in the genital area the first chakra receives its basic programming from our family and early experiences. This chakra regulates our physical needs - money, housing, food, and clothing. The first chakra is the source of passion - basic original feelings of rage, terror, joy, survival energy; material energy for achieving goals. The first chakra keeps our will to live alive. An imbalance in this chakra results in a feeling of insecurity. If there are not enough resources to provide adequate food, clothing or shelter among other things. The need of this chakra can be so consumed that you will find it difficult to focus on anything else. This chakra is your foundation.

## Below is some awareness on different levels of function.

**Overactive:** - Heaviness, sluggishness, slow movements, resistance to change, over eating, obesity, hoarding, material fixation, greediness, workaholic, and excessive spending.

**Low:** - Fear anxiety, resistance to structure, anorexia, underweight, feeling spacey, flightiness, vagueness, disconnection from your body, restlessness, inability to sit still, and difficulty manifesting.

**Balanced:** - Being grounded, good physical health, being comfortable in your body, a sense of safety and security, stability and solidity, right livelihood, prosperity, able to be still, and present in the here and now.

# Second Chakra
# Element: Water

Location: Pelvis Area - Below Your Navel
Color: Orange
Vibration: Pursuit of Pleasure - Desire & Sexuality

The primary drive of this center is the search for pleasure. It regulates sexual energy. It is the seat of creative expression. This is where you can experience the world as a magical place or not. This chakra is the source of feelings - emotions and our awareness of others, business ideas, all desires and sexual feelings. Water follows the path of least resistance and flows downward, following the shape of the earth or being absorbed into it. Where earth provides consistency, water induces change. Through change our consciousness begins to expand. Without water, growth is impossible. This energy center acts as our reproductive center for all areas of our lives and connects us with other life. An imbalance in this chakra can keep you searching for pleasure never feeling fulfilled. There can be a desire to lose yourself in sex, co-dependent relationships, drugs, alcohol, food or any stimulating sensation or jealously and developing over attachments.

# Below is some awareness on different levels of function.

**Overactive:** - Sexual addiction, obsessive attachments, addiction to stimulation, excessive mood swings, overly sensitive, poor boundaries, invasion of the personal space of others, and emotional dependency.

**Low:-** Rigidity in your body, beliefs or behavior, fear of change, emotional numbness or insensitivity, lack of desire, passion or excitement, avoidance of pleasure, fear of sexuality, poor social skills, boredom and excessive boundaries.

**Balanced:** - Graceful movement, ability to embrace change, emotional intelligence, ability to nurture self and others, healthy boundaries, ability to enjoy pleasure, passion, and sexual satisfaction.

# Third Chakra
# Element: Fire

Location: Solar Plexus Area
Color: Yellow
Vibration: Power & Will

This is the seat of personality. The third chakra plays an important part in a person's relationship with themselves and others. Our ability to connect, to belong, to make commitment to long-term intimate relationships, the love of people, animal, places and things are all associated with the third chakra. The drive of the third chakra assists one in being self-assertive, having a sense of power, recognizing yourself as an individual, develop principles you are willing to stand up for, the ability to support your boundaries, to say "yes" when you mean yes and "no" when you mean no, and the capacity to be able to make choices. An imbalance in the third chakra may result in the over use or under use of power, becoming too competitive, becoming ruthless which leads to a mistrust of life, a fear of letting go - believing that if you are not in control, things will not go your way, seeming to invite others to take advantage of you - playing the "martyr role" and the inability to assert yourself. These imbalances can lead to low self-esteem.

# Below is some awareness on different levels of function.

**Overactive: -** Dominating, controlling, competitive, arrogant, hyperactive, stubborn, ambitiously driven and compulsively focused towards goals (not caring how you achieve goals.)

**Low:-** Passivity, lack of energy, poor digestion, tendency to be cold, blaming, submissive, and low self esteem, lack of self worth and confidence, weak willpower, poor self discipline, cannot do things on own, needing someone to lean on for most things, like to use stimulants.

**Balanced:-**Resonant, full voice, clear communication with others, listen and act on inner knowing - inner calling, doing for one's self what is for your greater good, good listener, good timing. Lives life creatively, strong yet balanced will to follow through any decisions, assertiveness.

# Fourth Chakra
# Element: Fire

Location: The Heart
Color: Green and Pink
Vibration: Unconditional Love & Compassion

The path of the heart is unconditional love. When love is experienced there is warmth and joy. The opposite of love is fear. This vibration can assist you in magnetically attracting what you believe in - if you believe in abundance, than you will attract abundance. The heart chakra in balance can assists you in feeling at peace with yourself and the world. The heart is the seat of the soul. The source of the heart is positive healing energy, accomplishing our innermost desires, dreams, compassion and relationships. However, true relationship within the self should be achieved, before seeking a loving relationship with someone else. Hence the saying "loving yourself is the greatest love of all." The heart chakra contains the ability to relate. Love is the highest vibration in the Universe. The heart chakra is where the masculine and feminine energies merge creating a unity with the divine, when in positive balance. An imbalance in the heart charka may result in an over attachment in loving relationships, co-dependency, and the "bleeding heart" - unable to separate problems from those of others which make connection with others unhealthy and painful. This creates drama and issues that can sometimes keep us lost for many years. "I love you" is being said but "I need you" is what is meant.

## Below is some awareness on different levels of function.

<u>Overactive</u>: - Codependency (focusing too much on others), poor boundaries, jealousy, martyr, being a pleaser.

<u>Low</u>: - Antisocial, withdrawn, critical, intolerant, lonely, isolated, lack of empathy. Fear of intimacy. I love you is said - I need you is meant.

<u>Balanced</u>:- Caring, compassionate, kind, empathetic, accepting, self loving, peaceful, centered, being joyful and happy, taking care of one's needs, choosing to heal that which is of no value to the self, loves all of life, nature, seeing <u>all of life</u> as <u>one.</u>

# Fifth Chakra
# Element: Air

Location: The Throat
Color: Light Blue
Vibration: Communication and all Expressions

The fifth chakra is used for expression and for self-protection. Through this chakra we express what we think, feel, see, desire and do not like. This chakra can be called the "seat of responsibility" because it assists us in deciding our "yes" and "no" to life's choices.

This chakra is controlled by the higher mental place that allows detachment, observation, seeing, and understanding. The throat chakra moves you to express yourself in creative ways, not limited to speech like, writing, painting, dancing, music, thinking and any other form of expression. It is the source of all truths. The fifth chakra serves as an awakening of the upper three chakras, which are collective in nature and connects us to the higher dimension. It assists our species in questioning and knowing themselves; which serves as an evolutionary agent in the lives of all living beings. An imbalance in this chakra can result in opposing others' views because they choose to be contrary thus if everyone says "yes", these individuals will say "no", overwhelming opposition in order to validate their point of view, being a nonconformist or a rebel, being egotistic, challenging others views or being superficial.

# Below is some awareness on different levels of function.

<u>Overactive:</u>-Talking too much – or inappropriately, gossiping, stuttering, difficulty being silent, excessive loudness, inability to contain something told to you in confidence.

<u>Low:</u> - Difficulty putting things into words, fear of speaking out (<u>voice can be taking away in abusive</u> or <u>suppressing relationships/situations</u>), speaking with a small dainty weak voice, secretiveness, excessive shyness, tone deafness.

<u>Balanced:</u>- Resonant, full voice, clear communication with others, good communication with self, listens to inner voice, good listener, good sense of timing and rhythm, lives life creatively, knowing your purpose in life and being able to produce it in life, living life, and not let life, lives you.

# Sixth Chakra
# Element: Spirit

Location: Forehead
Color: Deep Blue
Vibration: Intuition and Perception

This chakra is also called the "third eye". It is our inner and outer visual center. Through this chakra we obtain, record and send pictures, symbols, colors and images that represent reality. Linked to the pituitary gland, this center regulates many of our hormonal and endocrine functions, basing physical health on our self-image and goals. The Yang aspect of this chakra relates to the ability to see and reach into the future. The Yin function relates to self-image and self-perception. This chakra has control over seeing into the higher planes; intuitive seeing, clairvoyance and other paranormal forms of knowing. The source of this chakra is insight, wisdom and creativity. It is the seat of vision and visioning. An imbalance in this chakra could result in getting lost in "non-reality" realness of the astral plane where fear, escapism, illusions and all other "imagination-run-wild" possibilities. Being engulfed by fear; where fear has its say in all the choices you make. Distorted vision and over reliance on drugs and alcohol can make this problem worse. Over-awareness of where you and others are in relation to spiritual development. For example, I do Reiki and she does not therefore I must be more spiritual. Spiritual development is not a competitive race.

Guilt which stems from a philosophical or religious belief, thinking there is a separation between self and the Divine can result in a belief that you are unworthy. Approach the sixth chakra in a sacred manner, this will provide a vehicle for your higher self to positively express itself to you. Your two visible eyes are like two lamps, assisting you physically, as you journey through life. Your third eye (the eye of the spiritual center) is the eye one should use for making life choices. Choice is the power of creation.

## Below is some awareness on different levels of function.

<u>Overactive</u>: - Hallucinations, delusions, obsessions, nightmares, intrusive memories, difficulty concentrating, excessive fantasizing.

<u>Low</u>: - Lack of imagination, difficulty visualizing, insensitivity, excessive skepticism, denial, inability to see alternatives, seeing yourself as better.

<u>Balanced</u>: - Strong intuition, penetrating insight, creative imagination, good memory, good dream recall, ability to visualize, has a guiding vision for life.

# Seventh Chakra
# Element: Spirit

Location: The Crown of the Head
Color: White/Purple
Vibration: Wisdom and Understanding

This chakra represents pure cosmic energy, the total surrender to Divine guidance. When the seventh chakra is opened and balanced you are awakened to the purpose of the soul for this life, and there is no denying your purpose. This knowledge carries a responsibility. Accept or deny it. There is a choice. If you deny your awareness of your purpose, again you will start to function again, using mostly your lower chakras; one, two and three. If you accept your purpose, you can tap more effortlessly into a positive source of energy that is perceived as infinite. All of the energy and circumstances that you desire to fulfill your soul's spiritual purpose will become available. The main source of this chakra is Divine awareness, and spiritual awakening. The female and male aspects of our being merge into oneness in both the sexes, in this chakra. The heart chakra mirrors the crown chakra in balance. It is the seat of our oneness with all creation, no separation, no different, and no better than any life in the Universe.

This chakra with the combination of the other chakras in balance opens to the highest vibration in the whole universe, which is LOVE. Unbalanced in the seventh chakra life will seem to be anchored in a separate reality, very real to you, but not integrated with the world around you. Confrontations with others and, fears will take center stage in your life. The "shopping list" mentalities of how you want your life to be, obsessively planning your life instead of letting life unfold spontaneously by choice. You will lack self-understanding and lack of direction. Feeling cluttered inside, which will eventually lead to cluttering in your physical life and environment.

## Below is some awareness on different levels of function.

**Overactive:** - Dissociation from your body, spiritual addiction, confusion, over – intellectualization, living in your head, disconnection from spirit, excessive attachment, seeing yourself as better, not integrated with the world around you, deep fears, shopping list mentality as to how you want things and life to be, feeling cluttered inside which leads to clutter in your physical life/environment.

**Low:** - Spiritual cynicism, a closed mind, learning difficulties, rigid belief system, apathy, lack of compassion and understanding.

**Balanced:** - Awake, spiritual connection, enlightenment, wisdom and mastery, intelligence, being present, open mindedness, ability to assimilate and seeing life in everything. Connected to the (I am.)

# Awareness of Balance

Working with the chakras requires internal balance. This can be achieved from inside with the assistance of choosing to healing personal experiences of suffering and trauma, correct thinking, positive speech, action, and loving kindness, to yourself and all living things. All of these help to produce unconditional love. With unconditional love, conflicts begin to transform from your life. You can then also improve not judging, defending and rationalizing experiences. This can assist with improving instincts of a reactionary point of view. Your life begins to work with great ease. Issues will continue to emerge, but you will be able to deal with them by making adjustments. Life will continue to unfold in mysterious ways. The unknown will always present new issues, challenging us in a never ending stream of opportunities, to evolve. "You never step into the same energy twice, there is always new energy flowing in." Once you learn the art of balancing your chakras you will be able to apply the same skill in each new situation.

Positive balance can bring a refinement to your life. Your senses of seeing, smelling, hearing, tasting, and feeling are heightened, and you are able to enjoy the most subtle experiences of life and living. It is as if each sense becomes easier to please. As you learn to center yourself, your senses become more refined, and it becomes easier to experience satisfaction at each of the chakras. Life's simple pleasures seem to bring more pleasant and joy filled experiences for you. More synchronicity and coincidences will also become a part of your life. It would seem like being in the effortless flow of positive life force energy.

"There is no way to love, love is the way." If you can find your way to positively balancing these energy centers one step at a time; things in your life can transform moment by moment from desperate needs to gracious opportunities, improved health and well being.

## Self help practices that can assist in positively balancing the Chakras.

### First Chakra

Imagine a grounding cord that runs from the spine deep into the earth. Imagine in your mind's eye an abundance of mental energy running down the spine, and dissipating through the grounding cord into the earth. Imagine the grounding cord growing roots, like giant trees. Picture the roots of the grounding cord intermingling with the roots of the giant trees. Now imagine that you can draw energy up from the earth, through your grounding cord. Picture the same centered strength of the tree being accessible to you, too. Grounding can also be cultivated by any activity that directly connects you to the earth like: gardening, hiking, slows walks, and walking barefoot on the earth.

## Second Chakra

In the middle of a hug, or while tasting something delightful, listening to beautiful music or witnessing an exquisite sunset, close your eyes for a moment and focus on the deep sense of satisfaction you are feeling. After experiencing an embrace with someone, close your eyes and enter into thankfulness for the experience, and focus on the delight of the sensations within your body. Notice that every cell in your body is alive with pleasure, joy, and sometimes a tingling vibration. Cultivate that sense of satisfaction. You will find that this leads to an awareness of fullness and completion.

## Third Chakra

If you are feeling overwhelmed and you find you are losing self-control, stop - breathe in and out four times, and activates your third chakra. Feeling overwhelmed always stem from the illusion that everything is happening at once. In truth, it is always just one moment at a time. Practice the art of being present in every moment, become aware of your breating in and breathing out.

Stop over booking schedules for yourself and your children. Stop having too much to do in any given time. Slow down and enjoy the moment. Manage time; do not let time manage you. Be an observer of things. Enjoy, see and Love the things you do. Accept the way people do things when you ask them, (it is their best), and it might not be your best. Love everything without condition. No strings attached. Enjoy the wind blowing through a tree, see the birds fly, enjoy it. These things happen no matter what is going on without condition. Love brings one into the light which assists you into moving more easily into your forth chakra (the heart). Learn meditation.

## Fourth Chakra

If you feel insecure about the object of love, realize that your issues are about security, not love. Go to the source of the problem. Go to the first chakra level. Go for a walk in nature and notice the inexhaustible life force all around you. Then feel the same life force moving through you too. Notice that you are not just living, life is living you, and living through you.

When you have established this feeling of security with yourself and life; you can enter a relationship fully. Rather than looking for security within the relationship, you would need to feel secure within yourself. Always remember love is the strongest force in the Universe. Forgiveness is perhaps the greatest attribute of the heart, awakened to compassionate love, which is universal love. When you give unconditional love you will receive, unconditional love. With this unconditional love, you should never experience burn out, because it becomes an exchange. Practice staying in your heart, so you do not put others out of your heart, and they will positively keep you in theirs.

## Fifth Chakra

Keep an open mind. This allows you to stay open to the process of discovery. Awaken to original insight; constantly look at life with fresh eyes. In relationships (personal/friends), use your insight to keep it growing like a plant, and constantly alive. Add fresh ideas into situations you are involved in. Keep promises, follow through with them, or do not make them at all. Do not promise things you have no control over, it might not work out the way you promised. This wastes time and energy. When you are in a group meeting or discussions, observe more than you speak. Listen and pay attention to other people and what they are saying. Be quiet and listen to things that are being said and the things that are not said. Hear yourself think.

Listen to animals and other things around you speak. Go to the ocean and listen to the waves. Go to the brook or a river, and listen to the new water rolling in. Speech and expression are alive and sacred.

## Sixth Chakra

An exercise to develop the Sixth Chakra is meditation. A simple meditation is by sitting quietly, in lotus, half lotus, kneeling or sitting on the front first half of a chair, with feet flat on the floor; palms turned up or down, one on each knee. Eyes opened or closed. Pay attention to your breath. You can say a simple mantra breathing in – breathing out. Focus on your breathing in and out; if your mind wanders away you bring your mind back to the awareness of breathing in and out.

# Seventh Chakra

Try to put your ego to rest, by transforming the negative emotional vibrations what is creating this ego perception attitude. To me the ego is fear based and means parts of someone mind consciousness has a strong reinforced negative imbalance attitude. This part of the person wants to keep pretending everything is personal priority, that they are spectacular, no matter if this is false or not. This created attitude will do everything to keep things in this false hallucination awareness. This ego attitude can create deep insecurity, low self esteem/value, and much imbalance in the person's chakras, spirit, mind, and body.

To learn and assist in improving the seventh chakra you can study the life of spiritual teachers, and masters. Practice seeing time as an ally, and not as an enemy. Learn to cherish the moment, and patience will blossom. Live time, do not let time live you. Trust in the path that leads you to inspiration and brings you closer to your higher self and the divine. Discover what your chosen life's purpose is.

Practice experiencing all things as one, same light different colors. Be in the world but not of the world. One very simple thing that can be very useful is to keep an open mind as much as possible.

An important reminder is - on this journey through life, you came with everything you will need for the journey. Choose to awaken, and make choices to live your best life today, in every moment, and in every breath. The spirit inside you will not awaken until you call it. This is your CHOICE.

# Bibliography and other recommended Chakra books are

Anodea Judith, Chakra Balancing, Sounds True, 2003.

Caroline Myss, PH.D, Anatomy of the Spirit, Three Rivers Press; NY, 1996.

Cyndi Dale, A New Chakra Healing, MN; Llewellyn 1999.

Keith Sherwood, Chakra Therapy, MN; Llewellyn 2000

# Afterword

In this outer realm of planet earth, humans can live and create helpful practices that transcend time and no time.

Yes, humans can live in harmonious relationships that support living in peace, love, harmony, joy, grace, and respect with all living things.

Yes, humans can assist in supporting the interconnected, infinite creation of awakened love and conscious light. One by one, we can make a big difference.

You can find useful treasures in family ancestral rites of passage, which can give life's journey new inspirational maps for living. Stop and take a look. You can find treasures in your own family and ancestral traditions. This is your choice.

The outer realm of a garden does not tell you what is inside. You have to enter a garden with curiosity, and explore to experience for yourself the music, and magic that lies within.

Like in a garden, take what you like and find useful from these stories, and leave the rest undisturbed. These are some of my favorite story creations that I choose to share with you. I love all the stories in this book.

Some people will say fairy tales are not real. What I will say is "if something is real to you, then it is real."

I also recommend reading fairy tales you like as often as possible. Reading fairy tales can assist in connecting to your inner child. All humans have an inner child.

A few of my fairytale books that I recommend are:-

**"My Big Book of Fairytales" by Peter Stevenson, and a Shaman symbolic tale story is "Skeleton Woman" by Alberto Villoldo.**

I enjoyed sharing my garden of stories with you. Thank you for reading my stories. Peace, blessings, and love to you.

Dorothea

# Biography

Dorothea Orleen Grant was born in Montego Bay, Jamaica West Indies. She has two children Renea, and Pia; and a granddaughter Ayanna. Currently, Dorothea uses her authentic talents and professional training in the holistic energy healing arts at Dogca Universal Wellness, a center she created in 2000. Dorothea works and lives in Midland Park, New Jersey, USA.

Throughout Dorothea's life, she loves to read. The art of storytelling and writing is also a natural talent and passion. She enjoys the magic of dreaming, and weaving vibrations with her writing skills from the non-physical to the physical, with the intention of taking people to places they might not be able to go in their normal human perception.

Dorothea is the author of "Enchantment Is Yours" A Journey of Spirit, "Chakras" Introduction to the Seven Major Energy

Centers, and two guided meditation CDs "Sacred Activation" and "Deep Relaxation."

# Notes

# Notes

# Notes

CPSIA information can be obtained at www.ICGtesting.com
Printed in the USA
BVOW04s1657100514

353104BV00002B/4/P

9 781452 593562